The Library Book Mystery

By Eleanor Robins

Development: Kent Publishing Services, Inc.
Design and Production: Signature Design Group, Inc.
Illustrations: Jan Naimo Jones

SADDLEBACK EDUCATIONAL PUBLISHING
Three Watson
Irvine, CA 92618-2767

Website: www.sdlback.com

ISBN-13: 978-1-59905-035-5
ISBN-10: 1-59905-035-8
e-book ISBN: 978-1-60291-460-5

Printed in China

12 11 10 09 08   9

Chapter 1

It was Monday. Lin was in science class. Miss Trent was her teacher.

Miss Trent said, "I graded your science tests. And I will give them back to you now. So you can find out what grade you got."

Lin thought she did well on her test.

Miss Trent gave Lin her paper.

Lin looked at her grade. She was right. She did do well on it.

Miss Trent gave Kris her paper.

Kris sat next to Lin.

Kris looked at her grade.

Then Kris looked at Lin. She said, "I got a 95 on my test. What did you get?"

"I got a 98," Lin said.

Lin always made the best grade in the class. And Kris always made the second best grade.

Miss Trent passed out the rest of the tests.

Then Miss Trent said, "You have to write a paper for this class. It should be five pages long. And it should be about a person."

"When is the paper due?" Lin asked.

"Friday of next week, Lin," Miss Trent said.

Kris said, "That doesn't give us much time."

Miss Trent looked at Kris. But she didn't say anything to her.

Miss Trent went to her desk. She picked up some papers.

Then Miss Trent said, "This is a list of people. Pick someone on the list.

But only one student can write about each person."

Miss Trent quickly passed out copies of the list.

Then she said, "Read the names. I will give you a few minutes to do that. Then I will call the roll. And you can tell me the person you picked."

Lin looked at the names. She knew who some of the people were. But she didn't know all of them.

Kris looked at the list of names, too. Then she looked at Lin.

Kris asked, "Who will you pick?"

Lin said, "I don't know yet. But it will be someone I want to learn more about."

Lin looked at the names for a few more minutes. Then she picked someone she liked.

Miss Trent called the roll.

The students told her who they had picked for their papers.

Miss Trent said, "Lin. Your turn."

Lin told Miss Trent the name of the person she had picked.

Miss Trent laughed.

Then Miss Trent said, "I should have known you would pick him, Lin. He will be a hard one to write about. It won't be easy to find out something about him. But I know you can do it. You always like to do hard work."

That made Lin feel very good.

Then Miss Trent said, "Kris, it is your turn."

Kris said, "I was going to write about that person. But Lin got to pick him first. Now I will have to pick someone else."

"That doesn't matter. Just do a good job on your paper," Miss Trent said.

Kris looked at the list of names. Then she picked someone else.

Lin thought Kris picked a good person. But Miss Trent didn't say anything about him.

Miss Trent called the names of the rest of the students. And they told her who they had picked.

Miss Trent said, "You might not find out a lot about your person. So you might have to pick someone else."

Lin hoped she could find a lot about her person.

"You have only two days to pick someone else. You can't change after that," Miss Trent said.

The bell rang.

Miss Trent said, "See you tomorrow. And don't forget to start to work on your papers."

All of the students had lunch next. They could leave their books on their desks until after lunch. It was OK with Miss Trent for them to do that.

Lin left her books on her desk. She started to walk to the door.

Lin wasn't in a hurry to leave. But Kris was. And Kris bumped into Lin.

Kris said, "Lin, watch where you are going."

Kris sounded mad. And she seemed mad, too.

Lin hoped Kris wasn't mad at her. But why would Kris be?

Chapter 2

Lin got to the lunchroom. She hurried inside. She got her lunch. Then she looked for her friends.

She saw Paige, Steve, and Carl. They sat at a table.

Lin lived at Grayson Apartments. The other three lived there, too. All four rode the same bus to school. And they were all good friends.

Lin hurried over to their table. She quickly sat down.

Lin told them she had to write a paper for science.

Steve said, "I am glad I don't have Miss Trent for science. I don't like to write papers."

"Me neither," Carl said.

"Who are you going to write about?" Paige asked.

Lin told her.

"I have never heard of him before," Paige said.

"His name was new to me, too. That is why I picked him. I want to learn about someone new," Lin said.

Jack came over to their table. Gail did, too.

Jack and Gail lived at Grayson Apartments, too. Jack rode the bus with Lin and the other three. Gail rode a special bus.

Lin told Jack and Gail about her paper. And she told them the person she had picked to write about.

Then Lin said, "I want to go to the library today. But I don't have time to go before school is out. I hope I find out a lot about him," Lin said.

Jack said, "I will be glad to drive you to the town library. We can go after school. Just say the word. And I will take you today."

Jack was the only one of them who had a car. It wasn't much of a car. But Jack liked to show it off. So he was always glad to take them somewhere.

"Thanks, Jack. I want to get started on my paper. But I can't go today," Lin said.

"I will be glad to look up something for you. I can do that today," Gail said.

Gail wanted to become a librarian. So she worked at the town library some days after school and some weekends.

Lin asked, "Will it be OK for you to do that?"

Gail said, "Sure. I just need to do library work while I am there. I will look for some books for you. And I will call you tonight. And let you know what I find."

"Thanks," Lin said.

Lin was glad Gail would look at the town library for her.

Maybe Gail would find something there to help her. Lin hoped she did.

Later, Gail looked for some books for Lin. But Gail didn't find what Lin needed. Lin found that out when Gail called her later that night.

Gail said, "I looked up that man for you, Lin. I found some books. They had a few things about him. But not anything that would help you a lot."

"Thanks for looking for me, Gail," Lin said.

"Sure. Any time," Gail said.

Lin would have to find a book at the school library. Or she would have to write about someone else. And she didn't want to do that.

Chapter 3

It was the next day. Lin was in science class. It was almost time for class to start.

Kris came over to her desk.

"I found what I need for my paper. Did you find what you need for your paper?" Kris asked.

Lin said, "Not yet. Gail looked at the town library for me. It doesn't have a lot about my person. And I haven't had time to go to the school library. I hope I find a lot about him."

"You might have to write about someone else," Kris said.

"I know. But I sure hope not, Kris," Lin said.

The bell rang. It was time for class to start. Miss Trent called the roll.

Then Miss Trent said, "Today we will go to the library. That will give you a chance to look up your person. And maybe check out some books."

Lin was glad to hear that.

Miss Trent said, "We will go now. So don't talk in the hall. And talk quietly when we get there."

The students went to the library.

Lin started to look for a book. She looked for a long time. She found some books. But they wouldn't help her very much.

Kris walked over to Lin.

Kris asked, "Did you find what you need for your paper?"

"Not yet. And I'm not sure I will," Lin said.

"That's too bad," Kris said. Then she walked away.

It was almost time for the class to be over. And then Lin found a book. It was just what she needed for her paper. Lin quickly checked the book out.

Lin wanted to show the book to Miss Trent. So she started to walk over to Miss Trent.

Kris hurried over to Lin.

Kris asked, "Did you find something you can use for your paper?"

"Yes," Lin said.

"Let me see it," Kris said.

Lin showed her the book. But she didn't know why Kris wanted to see it.

The bell rang. Lin had to go to lunch. So she didn't have time to show the book to Miss Trent. But that was OK. She could show the book to Miss Trent later.

Lin got all of her things. She walked to the door. Kris did, too. Kris was in a hurry. She bumped into Lin.

Kris said, "Watch what you are doing, Lin. And don't bump into me."

Lin wanted to say she didn't bump into Kris. But Kris sounded mad. Was Kris mad at Lin?

Chapter 4

It was the next day. Lin was in science class. It was almost time for class to start.

Lin wanted to show her book to Miss Trent. But Kris said something to Lin before she could.

Kris asked, "Did you get a lot done on your paper last night?"

Lin said, "No. I didn't. I had to study for a math test. But I hope to get a lot done on it tonight."

Kris didn't seem mad. So it must be a good day for Kris. And Lin was glad about that.

Lin asked, "How about you? Did you get a lot done on your paper?"

"Yes," Kris said.

The bell rang. And Miss Trent started class.

Then Miss Trent said, "You can work on your papers all period. You can start on them now. You need to work. Don't talk to each other. This isn't a free period."

That was OK with Lin. She didn't want to talk. She just wanted to work on her paper.

Miss Trent said, "I will call each of you to my desk. And you can tell me about the books that you found. But first, does anyone need to pick someone else? Today is the last day you can do that."

No one needed to do that. So all of the students got busy. Or at least they acted as if they were busy.

The students went over to Miss Trent, one at a time.

Then Miss Trent said, "Lin. It is your turn."

Lin walked over to Miss Trent. She had her library book.

"This is what I found, Miss Trent," Lin said.

Lin gave her book to Miss Trent. Miss Trent looked at the book. Then she gave it back to Lin.

Miss Trent said, "I am glad you picked your person, Lin. You should learn a lot about him from this book."

"I hope I do," Lin said.

And Lin thought she would.

Miss Trent said, "I will enjoy reading your paper, Lin."

That made Lin feel very good. And she was glad she picked that person.

Lin went back to her desk. She worked some more on her paper.

Then the end of class bell rang.

Miss Trent said, "Time to go. Don't forget to work on your papers tonight."

Lin got up to go to lunch. She left her books on her desk. Lin walked to the door.

Kris seemed like she was mad again.

But Lin didn't know why. Lin hadn't done anything to Kris. So Kris couldn't be mad at her. Maybe it was just a bad week for Kris.

Kris wasn't in a hurry to leave. And Lin was glad. She didn't want Kris to bump into her again.

Lin walked into the lunchroom. She got her lunch. Then she saw Paige and Gail. They were at a table.

Lin hurried over to their table and sat down.

Gail asked, "Did Miss Trent let you work on your paper today?"

Lin said, "Yes. And I got a lot done."

"Good. Maybe you will finish it this weekend," Paige said.

"I hope so. But I need to get a lot done tonight," Lin said.

The girls started to talk about other things. And they talked too long.

Then Paige asked, "What time is it? I left my watch at home."

Lin looked at her watch.

She said, "Oh, no. We need to go. Or we will be late to class."

Lin quickly got up from the table. She took her tray back. Then she hurried into her science class to get her books.

Lin was in a hurry to go to her next class. So she didn't make sure all of her books were on her desk. She just quickly put them in her backpack.

Lin didn't think about the book she needed for the science report again until she got home. Then she looked in her backpack to get her book. It wasn't there.

Someone had taken her book when she was at lunch.

But why would someone steal her book? No one else needed it for the science report.

Chapter 5

It was the next morning. Lin was at the bus stop. Paige was there. Steve and Jack were there, too.

Lin was very upset. She didn't know where her book was. And she didn't get to work on her paper the night before.

Steve said, "You don't look so good, Lin. What is wrong with you?"

Lin wanted to do well on her schoolwork. So she always worried about it.

"Are you sick?" Paige asked.

Lin said, "No, Paige. But I am in big trouble."

Maybe it wasn't big trouble for Paige. But it seemed like it was to Lin.

"Why? What did you do, Lin?" Steve asked.

"I didn't do anything," Lin said.

"So what is the problem then?" Steve asked.

"That book I checked out of the library. The one for my paper. I can't find it. And now I can't work on my paper," Lin said.

"When did you first miss the book?" Paige asked.

Lin said, "Last night. When I got ready to work on my paper."

"Did you look all around your house for it?" Paige asked.

"Yes. That is what I would have done," Jack said.

"I didn't need to do that. I just opened my backpack. And my book wasn't there," Lin said.

"Where was the last place you saw it? Maybe you didn't take it to school yesterday," Steve said.

Lin said, "I did take it. I showed it to Miss Trent. And I used it to work on my paper in class."

Paige said, "You just took it to some other class. So your book must be in that class."

"Yeah. You just forgot where you left it," Steve said.

"For sure," Jack said.

"No. I didn't take it to another class. I think someone took it," Lin said.

They all seemed surprised.

"That is a dumb thing to say, Lin. Why would someone take your book?" Steve asked.

"Yes. Why would someone take your book?" Jack asked.

"I don't know. But I think someone did," Lin said.

"You must be wrong, Lin. You are the only one who needs it. You must have put it somewhere. And you just forgot where," Paige said.

Lin said, "No. I didn't. My book was on my desk when I went to lunch. It was gone when I got back."

"You should have said something then," Steve said.

"That is what I would have done," Jack said.

"I told you. I didn't know it was gone until I got home," Lin said.

"Then it has to be at school. In a classroom. Or maybe someone picked it up. But they didn't mean to do that," Paige said.

"Yeah," Steve said.

"Just say the word. And I will help you look for it," Jack said.

"Thanks, Jack," Lin said.

"We will all help," Paige said.

"And I will tell Carl and Gail, too," Jack said.

"Tell us the name of the book. So we will know what to look for," Steve said.

Lin told them.

Then Lin said, "We have to find it. I really need it to make a good grade on my paper."

The bus came. And they climbed onto the bus.

"Don't worry, Lin. One of us will find your book," Paige said.

"Yeah," Steve said.

"For sure," Jack said.

Lin knew they didn't think someone stole the book. They thought she just left it somewhere. And she just forgot where she left it. So they thought the book wouldn't be hard to find.

Chapter 6

The bus got to school. Lin got off the bus. She hurried into the school. She wanted to see Miss Trent before school started.

Lin walked quickly down the hall.

Kris called to her.

Kris asked, "Why are you in a hurry, Lin? Where are you going?"

"I want to see Miss Trent," Lin said.

"Why?" Kris asked.

But Lin wanted to see Miss Trent. And she didn't have time to tell Kris.

Lin got to Miss Trent's room. Miss Trent was in her room. And Lin was very glad.

Lin said, "I need to talk to you, Miss Trent."

Miss Trent said, "You seem upset, Lin. What is wrong?"

"My book is missing. The one I need for my paper," Lin said.

Lin didn't want to say it was stolen.

Miss Trent seemed surprised.

Miss Trent said, "I am very surprised, Lin. You are a very good student. And I never thought you would lose a book."

"I didn't lose it. Someone took it," Lin said.

She still didn't want to say someone stole it.

Miss Trent seemed even more surprised by what Lin said.

Miss Trent said, "I can't believe someone would take your book. Why do you think that, Lin?"

"The book was on my desk when I went to lunch. It was gone when I got back," Lin said.

"Why didn't you tell me then?" Miss Trent asked.

"I didn't know it was missing then. I didn't miss it until I got home," Lin said.

"Then you don't know when you lost it," Miss Trent said.

Lin wanted to tell Miss Trent again that she didn't lose it. But she didn't. She knew Miss Trent wouldn't believe her.

"You must have left it somewhere at school, Lin. Look for it in your other classes. And maybe you will find it. And look again at home. It might be there," Miss Trent said.

Lin knew it wasn't at home. And she knew it wasn't in her other classes.

Someone took it.

But who?

And why did the person take it?

But most of all, where was her book?

Miss Trent said, "I will tell all of my students about your book. And I will ask if they have seen it. They will let you know if they know where it is, Lin."

"Thank you, Miss Trent," Lin said.

But Lin didn't think that would help her much.

Lin was worried only one person knew where the book was. The person who stole it. And Lin didn't think that person would tell where it was.

"What am I going to do? Can I pick someone else to write about, Miss Trent?" Lin asked.

Lin didn't want to do that. But she knew she should.

Miss Trent said, "I am sorry, Lin. But it is too late for you to do that. Yesterday was the last day to change your person."

But Lin had to write about someone else for her paper.

Lin said, "But I don't have my book. And I need it to make a good grade on my paper."

"I am sorry, Lin," Miss Trent said. And she did seem sorry.

Miss Trent said, "I can't let you pick someone else. That wouldn't be fair to your classmates. You lost your book. They didn't lose their books."

Lin went to the door. She was very upset now. She had to find her book.

Lin walked out in the hall. She saw Kris. Kris was standing just outside Miss Trent's room.

Lin almost bumped into her. Kris had a big smile on her face.

Kris said, "So you lost your book. Too bad."

But Kris didn't seem like she thought it was too bad.

Lin started to say she didn't lose her book. That someone took it. But Kris spoke before she could.

Kris said, "You always make the best grade. But this time you won't, Lin. Not without that book."

Kris still had a big smile on her face. Then Kris hurried off.

Kris must have stolen the book. Lin was almost sure about that.

But she didn't think Kris would say she did. And Lin couldn't prove it.

So how could Lin get her book back from Kris?

Chapter 7

Later that morning, Lin was in the lunchroom. She looked for her friends.

Lin saw Steve. He was at a table with a girl. She must be his new girlfriend. Steve liked to date many girls.

Then Lin saw Gail and Paige. They sat at a table. Carl and Jack were with them, too.

Lin got her lunch. Then she hurried over to the table and sat down.

Gail asked, "Did you find your book, Lin?"

"No," Lin said.

Paige said, "Sorry, Lin. I asked

around. But I didn't find out anything about your book."

"And I looked in all the desks I saw," Jack said.

"Me, too. And I also looked in the gym," Carl said.

"Thanks to all of you for the help. We didn't find my book. But I might know who took it," Lin said.

"Who did?" all four asked at the same time.

Lin told them she talked to Kris. And she told them what Kris had said about her book.

"Kris must have taken it," Carl said.

"For sure," Jack said.

Gail said, "You shouldn't say that, Jack. She might have taken it. But we don't know that for sure."

"What can I do? Just say the word. And I will do it," Jack said.

"Just keep looking for my book. And ask some more people about it," Lin said.

"We will, Lin. And we will find it," Paige said.

"Yes. We will," Gail said.

But Lin didn't think they would. At least not before her paper was due.

Paige said, "We can hurry and eat. And then go and talk to people about the book."

"That sounds like a plan to me," Carl said.

"And to me," Jack said.

They all ate quickly. And they didn't talk.

Then all five left the lunchroom. Lin and Gail went out into the hall. They hurried down the hall.

Lin and Gail saw Kris. She was walking in front of them.

Gail said, "Wait, Kris. We want to talk to you."

Kris stopped. Then she turned around to face them.

Kris asked, "What do you want? I didn't do anything wrong."

"I didn't say you did," Gail said.

"So what do you want?" Kris asked.

Gail said, "Lin can't find her library book. Do you know where it is?"

"How would I know? Lin needs to keep track of her books. Maybe then she wouldn't lose them," Kris said.

"I didn't lose my book. Someone took it," Lin said.

Gail said, "That is right. And we thought you might know who took it."

"How would I know?" Kris asked.

"Maybe because you took it. So then Lin wouldn't make a good grade on her paper. And you would make the best grade, not Lin," Gail said.

Kris looked at them. She seemed mad. At first she didn't say anything.

But then Kris said, "Maybe I took the book. Maybe I didn't. But what if I did? You can't prove it. And you will never find it. Not where I would have put it."

Then Kris hurried off.

"She took it. I know she took it," Lin said.

"I think she did, too," Gail said.

"But how can we prove it?" Lin asked Gail.

"I don't think we can," Gail said.

"What am I going to do? I have to get my book back before next Friday," Lin said.

Gail said, "I know. But don't give

up. We still have some time to look for it, Lin."

"But where is it?" Lin asked.

"I don't know. But we will think of somewhere," Gail said.

They might think of somewhere else to look. But Lin didn't think her book would be there.

Chapter 8

Lin and Gail were still in the hall. They were trying to think of a place to look for Lin's book.

Gail asked, "Have you been to the library today, Lin? Have you asked about your book?"

"No," Lin said.

"We have some time before our next class. We can go there now. Maybe someone found your book. And turned it in," Gail said.

"OK," Lin said.

The two girls went to the library.

Lin asked if her book had been turned in. But it hadn't been turned in.

That didn't surprise Lin. She didn't think it had been.

The girls left the library. They hurried down the hall.

Lin was sure she wouldn't find the book. So she wouldn't make a good grade on her paper.

Gail stopped her wheelchair.

Lin asked, "What is wrong, Gail?"

Gail quickly turned her wheelchair around.

Then Gail said, "I have an idea. Come on."

Gail started to move her wheelchair quickly down the hall. Lin hurried to keep up with her.

"Where are we going?" Lin asked.

"To the library," Gail said.

"Why? We were just there. And no one had turned in my book," Lin said.

"And I don't think anyone will turn it in," Gail said.

"Why?" Lin asked.

Gail was in a hurry. So she didn't answer Lin.

The two girls got to the library.

Gail asked, "Do you know the call number of your book?"

"No," Lin said.

But Lin knew what a call number was. It let people know where a book could be found in the library.

Gail said, "Quick. Look up the call number of your book. Then write it down. And bring it to me. I can guess some of the call number. But I need to know all of it."

"OK," Lin said.

Gail wheeled over to look at some of the books.

Lin quickly found the call number of her book. And she took it to Gail.

Gail looked at the call number. Then she looked at the shelf in front of her.

"Found it," Gail said.

Gail got a book off of the shelf. She gave the book to Lin.

Lin couldn't believe it. It was her missing book.

"How did you know it was here?" Lin asked.

Gail said, "I didn't know for sure. But Kris said it was somewhere we would never look."

And Lin would never have looked there at all.

"Kris thought we would only ask if the book had been turned in. And we wouldn't look on the shelf. So I thought Kris might have put it here," Gail said.

"But how did you think to look here? I would never have thought to do that," Lin said.

Gail said, "I work in a library. I know that sometimes a book is on the shelf. But we think it is checked out. That doesn't happen a lot. But it is a good idea to look on the shelf. And make sure the book isn't there."

"I am glad you work at the town library, Gail. So you knew to look on the shelf for my book. Kris put the book on the shelf. But she didn't check it in. It was the perfect hiding place," Lin said.

Lin was sure Kris put her book on the shelf. But Lin couldn't prove it. So she wouldn't say anything to Kris about the book.

Lin was just glad that Gail found the book for her. And now she thought she would make a good grade on her paper for Miss Trent.

MONTRÉAL ON FOOT

WITH

IVAN DROUIN

URBAN STORYTELLER

UNDERGROUND MONTRÉAL

Sgräff

4

6

8

24

44

63

FOREWORD

INTRODUCTION

TOUR 1
Downtown: a walk through Montréal's retail roots

TOUR 2
International Quarter:
exploring Montréal's corridors of design

TOUR 3
Entertainment district: footsteps towards
cultural Montréal

CONCLUSION

FOREWORD

Only after visiting other countries and speaking to tourists in Montréal does it become apparent what a mystery the underground city is for many people. No one seems to know exactly what it is or how to get in, and all are afraid of losing their way! As a certified Montréal tour guide, I often take visitors around this fascinating network. It's my pleasure to share some of these circuits with you in this guide, and to let you in on some of the secrets they hold.

Originally from the Beauce region, I completed a Bachelor's degree in business administration, major in tourism, at UQAM in 1977 and then travelled the world as a professional tour guide and explorer for over fifteen years. I finally decided to settle in Montréal, a city I didn't know very well at the time, and set about discovering it through a visitor's eyes. I explored the streets and back alleys of every district. I fell in love with the city's diversity, its atmosphere, its

history—or rather the many stories making up its history. I wanted others to be able to discover this city with the same fascination and curiosity as me, using all the senses, highlighting what makes it so attractive and learning to appreciate its flaws.

Thus Kaleidoscope Tours (www.tourskaleidoscope.com) was born, to allow everyone to discover the rich diversity of the neighbourhoods, cultures, and heritage that make up Montréal. I am proud to be an ambassador of this very special city.

So, please follow me!

INTRODUCTION

Montréal's indoor pedestrian network is the most extensive and diverse in the world. The curiosity it attracts is the envy of many major cities. Yet, as with all familiar places, its users no longer pay it much attention. I'm going to show you the more intriguing features of this unique complex that bear testimony to the challenges, dreams, and entrepreneurial spirit of the builders and inhabitants of Montréal.

But what exactly is this "underground city"? Well, let's put one thing straight: people don't actually live down there. Montrealers aren't moles or characters in some futuristic novel; on the contrary, they love spending time outdoors in their city! In fact, it's more of a parallel world, a system of interlacing passages, tunnels, and indoor spaces that allow pedestrians to circulate between the downtown sector and Old Montréal, and which has expanded with the Metrosystem※.

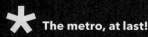

The metro, at last!

In Québec, work began after the Quiet Revolution to build an entirely underground Metro that would run on pneumatic tires. Three lines and 20 stations were inaugurated in October 1966. Today, Montréal's Metro system comprises four lines and 68 stations.

The busiest section is called the RÉSO*, and you'll see this sign above some Metro entrances. Montrealers especially appreciate the indoor network for the year-round protection it affords from the extremes of their weather. I love being able to walk around town in a pair of lightweight shoes in the middle of February!

I've put together three circuits, covering the downtown area, the international quarter, and the entertainment district respectively, each taking between one and two hours, depending on your pace and how often you stop. You can do them separately, or easily link them up, which makes about 5 km (3 miles) in all. So, put on your comfiest walking shoes and let's set off on an urban safari to explore the depths of Montréal—without getting lost!

The RÉSO

Used by over half a million people every day, Montréal's indoor network, branded the RÉSO, is made up of some 32 km (20 miles) of pedestrian corridors connecting more than 200 access points, 10 metro, train and bus stations, around 100 office and university buildings, and over 2,000 shops and restaurants.

TOUR 1
DOWNTOWN: A WALK THROUGH MONTRÉAL'S RETAIL ROOTS

START
Metro: Peel, exit "Peel Sud" towards Cours Mont-Royal

END
Metro: Bonaventure, Central Station

REFERENCE POINTS

ARCHITECTURE
Atrium – Complexe Les Ailes

ART
Solstice – Carrefour Industrielle Alliance

ENTERTAINMENT
Grévin Museum – Eaton Centre

RESTAURANT
Katz's Delicatessen – Place Ville Marie

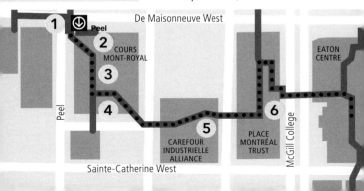

1

Ceramic designs – 54 circles, by Jean-Paul Mousseau

On this tour I'll explain how the creators of the indoor city used natural light to create a pleasant and welcoming environment so users would not feel claustrophobic. As we walk, you'll get a better understanding of how the network expands outwards from this downtown core.

■ **Peel metro station**

Our walk begins inside the station on a large circle of coloured tiles, one of which is signed. You're standing on a piece of artwork: *Ceramic designs – 54 circles* (1964), by **Jean-Paul Mousseau**, who was a student of Paul-Émile Borduas. There are many such circles throughout this station and all are unique; one of the larger ones, above a platform, is dedicated

De Maisonneuve West

1 Peel

2 COURS MONT-ROYAL

3

4

Peel

5 CARREFOUR INDUSTRIELLE ALLIANCE

6 PLACE MONTRÉAL TRUST

McGill College

EATON CENTRE

Sainte-Catherine West

2

Cours Mont-Royal:
staircase

3

Cours Mont-Royal:
tropical garden

4

Majestic
chandelier,
imported from
the Monte-Carlo
casino

Underground Montréal

2

to the artist's wife. If you count them all, you'll find 37. Originally there were 54, but some had to be removed due to renovation work.

Exit the metro station, following signs for Cours Mont-Royal.

■ Cours Mont-Royal

When you come into the first inner court, take the large grey-green staircase to your left. Ahead is a delightful **tropical garden** that's worth stopping to admire. Take the escalator behind the staircase up to the second level, then turn right. If you look up you'll see a series of hanging **bird-people sculptures**, or *tingmiluks*, by the prominent Inuit artist David Ruben Piqtoukun. They represent winged shamans endowed with the gift of flight by the Inuit spirit and god of

3

4

Historical note

Built in 1922, the Mount Royal Hotel was designed in the Beaux-Arts style with neo-Georgian and neo-baroque features. With over a thousand rooms, it was the largest hotel in the British Empire, and it was said that one could *be born and die there without ever leaving...*

5

Solstice by Guido Molinari

6

Grand atrium of Place Montréal Trust

wind, Sila. A little further on, under the decorative ceiling, hangs a **majestic chandelier**, imported from the Monte-Carlo casino, recreating the splendour of the days when this was the Mount Royal Hotel . After the hotel closed in 1983, the building was converted to offices and a shopping centre with international and designer brands.

Continue to the end of the promenade and turn left, to take an escalator and then a large grey staircase down to the Metro level again. You'll see a food court ahead of you. To continue your tour, take the "Cours Mont-Royal" passage, to your left, towards the Carrefour Industrielle Alliance.

■ **Carrefour Industrielle Alliance**

When you arrive in this complex, take the escalator leading up into

Anecdote

The prestigious McGill College Avenue was very nearly sold to a promoter who wanted to cover it with a glass roof and install boutiques and a concert hall. The mayor at the time, Jean Drapeau, approved the transaction, but city residents banded together to stop the project from going ahead.

Simons department store, and on your way up, admire the large geometric sculpture hanging overhead. Entitled *Solstice* (1999), this is the work of **Guido Molinari**, who was one of Québec's leading figures in abstract art. This brightly coloured mobile made entirely of translucent acrylic symbolizes the passing of the fashion seasons and was put in motion by the industrial designer **Michel Dallaire**.

Head back down and continue towards Place Montréal Trust, to the right.

■ Place Montréal Trust

You will arrive in the **grand atrium** mall, of Brutalist, natural, minimalist design. Its glass roof visually opens up the space, and in its centre stands a tall copper fountain, the *Indoor Fountain* (1988) by **Zeidler Roberts**, which boasts one of the highest indoor water spouts in North America. During the Holiday season, the fountain is turned into an interactive multimedia Christmas tree.

Walk round the left-hand side of the atrium to reach the gallery opposite, towards the information booth. On the way, you'll pass a branch of **Omer DeSerres**, a family-owned arts and creative leisure supplies company founded in 1908. Take the tunnel that runs under McGill College Avenue to the Eaton Centre .

■ Eaton Centre

Head towards the central hall and turn right along the passage until you get to the glass elevator

a few metres further on. Travel up to the 5th floor to the **Grévin Museum**, where you can see over a hundred waxwork figures of well-known personalities from Québec and around the world who have marked our history, culture, and society. An immersive and entertaining experience, with plenty of amusing photo opportunities! Stop off at the museum gift shop and don't miss the Café Grévin, headed by acclaimed Montréal chef **Jérôme Ferrer**. I especially recommend his tasty and affordable lunch boxes and his delicious fresh-baked macaroons.

7

Café Grévin

Before heading back down, take the time to admire the impressive multi-storey structure✶ and magnificent glass canopy by **Peter Rose**, for which he received an award from Québec's architects' association in 1991. The Montréal-based architect also designed the Canadian Centre for Architecture.

8

Glass canoy by Peter Rose

9

Murals by Maurice Savoie

Take the elevator back down to the Metro level (2), walk to the other side of the centre, following signs for McGill metro station, and go into the station.

✶ Not for the faint-hearted!

Opened in 1976, the Eaton Centre was originally called Les Terrasses and was designed on a model advocated by consumption spin doctors that obliged shoppers to circulate and therefore spend money. But people didn't like its complicated, maze-like layout and stayed away! In 1986, the mall was renamed, the layout was gradually simplified, and it was renovated according to the latest trends—as decreed by the experts.

9

■ McGill metro station

Walk up to the doors leading to the Complexe Les Ailes, on the right. This busy station is located right in the heart of town and serves the many surrounding offices and shopping malls, as well as the university of the same name. It houses several works of art, including, on either side of these doors, *Murals* (1966) by **Maurice Savoie**, fine terra cotta low-relief murals depicting flowers, leaves, and creatures.

Now take the crossing opposite to reach the walkway on the other side. If you look down to the platforms below, you'll see five stained-glass murals by **Nicolas Sollogoub**. *Montréal Scenes Circa 1830* (1964-1969) depicts aspects of life in 19th century Montréal: the Chapelle Notre-Dame-de-Bon-Secours; the Sulpician Seminary; mayors Jacques Viger and Peter McGill, and the city's former coat of arms; John Molson's steamship and some of the economic activities of the time.

Underground Montréal

15

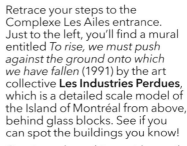

10
Exibit on the Anglican Christ Church Cathedral

11
Bust of Raoul Wallenberg

12
KPMG building

10

Retrace your steps to the Complexe Les Ailes entrance. Just to the left, you'll find a mural entitled *To rise, we must push against the ground onto which we have fallen* (1991) by the art collective **Les Industries Perdues**, which is a detailed scale model of the Island of Montréal from above, behind glass blocks. See if you can spot the buildings you know!

Continue along this corridor until you come to the entrance of the Promenades Cathédrale, on the right.

■ **Promenades Cathédrale**

Go through the doors, take a left and then a right, to see an exhibit presenting the remarkable history of the **Anglican Christ Church Cathedral**, an emblem of Montréal's religious heritage and the city's oldest English-speaking parish . . . and the temple of retail—the Promenades Cathédrale shopping mall—that lies directly beneath it✱!

Head down the corridor, turn into the next passage you come to on the right, and continue to the next intersection.

✱ Historical note

Based on the model of Salisbury Cathedral in England, Christ Church Anglican Cathedral was built in 1859, but not long after, it began to subside due to the soft, marshy ground. The stone steeple was subsequently removed to prevent further damage, and was replaced 15 years later by one made of aluminium. Since 1987, the cathedral has been held up by 21 structural pillars and is no longer sinking. A feat of technical genius!

For a bit of fresh air and a change of scenery at this point, you can go up the escalator on your right, which will lead you out behind the KPMG building into a quiet garden, **Raoul Wallenberg square**, dedicated to the memory of a diplomat who saved thousands of Jews during World War II. Notice how the windows in the courtyard imitate the shapes of the arches on the cathedral.

To continue with your tour, go straight ahead and enter Complexe Les Ailes.

■ Complexe Les Ailes

Take the escalator down to ground level (Rez-de-chaussée). Created in 1999, the interior spaces and **columned galleries** of this shopping complex are grandiose, reminiscent of Galeries Lafayette in Paris, Macy's in New York, or Harrods in London⋆. Unfortunately, the economic downturn following the events of September 11, 2001 took its toll on the luxury boutiques, and in 2007, the complex adopted a more modest retail approach and also now has offices on the upper floors.

⋆ Historical note

Built in 1925, the building that now houses Complexe Les Ailes was originally home to Eaton's, a retail department store, and its famous restaurant, The Ninth Floor, whose art deco dining room was modelled on that of the *Île-de-France* ocean liner. This space has been preserved, but it is no longer accessible to the public.

McGill

COMPLEXE LES AILES

EATON CENTRE

KPMG BUILDING 10

11 12

14

13

PROMENADES CATHÉDRALE

McGill College

Sainte-Catherine

13

13

Columned galleries of Complexe Les Ailes

14

Statue of Maurice Richard

Take the escalator up to the Mezzanine level, where you'll see a statue of **Maurice Richard, AKA "The Rocket"**, entitled *Never Give Up* (1999-2001)—the player's motto—created by **Jean-Raymond Goyer** and **Sylvie Beauchêne**. This hockey legend led the Montréal Canadiens to eight Stanley Cup wins, an exploit we're not likely to see repeated anytime soon! A little further on, take a closer look at the reproductions of old photos on the columns of the adjoining gallery that relate part of Montréal's manufacturing history.

Now go back down to the Metro level and make your way towards the Eaton Centre again, to the right. You'll pass a "Signature" store of the **Société des alcools du Québec** (SAQ), selling a wide range of wines and spirits. Their cellar is situated in what used to be a bank vault. If you're looking for a rare cognac, look

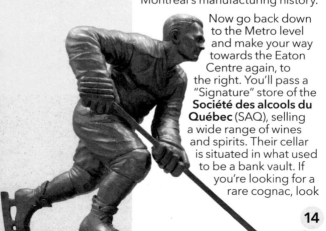

14

15

15

Place Ville Marie

no further. Unless you'd prefer a Québec or Canadian specialty like Caribou, locally produced wine, maple liqueur, ice or fire cider, or other such heady delights. Don't hesitate to ask the staff for advice!

■ **Eaton Centre**

Back in the Eaton Centre, take the left-hand escalator down to the Tunnel level. Behind the escalator you'll see a passage leading to **Place Ville Marie**. This tunnel wasn't opened to the public until more than fifteen years after it was built. The private owners of the surrounding buildings had to reach agreements on cleaning and maintenance, safety and security, and corridor access. And yet this was a critical portion of the network because it completed the pedestrian link between the orange and green metro lines, and between the train and bus stations.

At the end of the long corridor, take the escalator up to the shopping promenade in Place Ville Marie. If you turn around at this point, you can check up on the weather outside!

■ **Place Ville Marie**

Walk on to the next intersection.

Taking the escalator directly in front of you will lead you on a short detour to admire the plain but imposing lobby of this iconic building and the works of art there.

Walk down the main pedestrian corridor on the right and stop at the entrance to the food court. The large windows overhead provide a **spectacular view of the main tower of Place Ville Marie**.

This complex marks the realization of Montréal's vision in the 1960s, which was to make its downtown area a retail and commercial hub, and it has a remarkable story. On this spot an enormous trench had been dug for the railway tracks that would connect the tunnel bored through Mount Royal in 1918 with the Central Station. The city centre lay thus disfigured for 30 years before the **Canadian National Railway (CN)** and **William Zeckendorf**, an American promoter, agreed on plans for the site: a cruciform tower structure that would let in a maximum amount of light, designed by **Ieoh Ming Pei**, the architect who went on to create the Louvre Pyramid in Paris. When it was inaugurated in 1962, Place Ville Marie was the tallest skyscraper in the Commonwealth, and rapidly became emblematic of the city ✳.

Go up the steps, which will take you outside.

■ **Place Ville Marie** esplanade

This huge paved public area has a splendid **view over McGill College Avenue and Mount Royal Park**. Here you'll find a **compass rose**, a bronze sculpture by **Gerald**

 Anecdote

Then Mayor Jean Drapeau insisted that the new complex be given a French name. The promoter suggested "centre de la Réforme" (Reformation Centre) or "place de la Renaissance" (Renaissance Place), but the mayor imposed "Place Ville Marie" as a reminder of the city's first name.

✱ The saga of a name

Completed in 1958, the Queen Elizabeth Hotel was one of the first hotels in North America to have escalators, central air conditioning, and a telephone in every room. The Governor General of Canada travelled to England to request authorization from the Queen to name the new hotel after her. This irked the Québec nationalists, who preferred the name Château Maisonneuve, in memory of the city's founder. But despite all their petitions and attempts to influence Mayor Drapeau, the hotel kept its name.

16

Compass rose

17

Self-Portrait by **Nicolas Baier**

Gladstone called *Feminine Presence* (1972), as well as *Self-Portrait* (2012) by **Nicolas Baier**, a tempered glass cube containing a conference table and various nickel chrome objects, marking the building's 50th anniversary.

To the south is the **Fairmont The Queen Elizabeth Hotel** ✱, whose distinguished guests have included Queen Elizabeth II, Indira Gandhi, Charles de Gaulle, Nelson Mandela, the Dalai Lama, and, most memorably, **John Lennon**, who in 1969 held his famous "bed-in" there with Yoko Ono to protest against the war in Vietnam and recorded the classic *Give Peace a Chance*.

Go back down to the food court. Between the staircases, in a corner, is **Katz's Delicatessen**, a traditional deli with take-out service for those who'd like to try the famous Montréal-style smoked meat, a Jewish specialty. Continue following the passage on the right, following signs to Central Station, whose shopping area you'll reach after going down another escalator.

■ Central Station

You're now in the "Halles de la gare" shopping and restaurant area. Follow the main walkway, where you should have no trouble finding something tasty to eat, perhaps from the tempting selection of sweet and savoury delights at the excellent **Première Moisson bakery**, a Québec-based business that promotes local produce. At the end of this passage, you'll arrive in the main station concourse.

The underground pedestrian network originally started from this point, and its subsequent development led to the migration of the financial district from Old Montréal towards McGill College Avenue. Construction of the Central Station was completed in 1943. Its architecture was to have been based on the Rockefeller Center in New York, but under the influence of the modernist trends of the day, the result was more of a facade-less concrete cube. It was a revolutionary design at the time, with its innovative **waiting area** located above the platforms but on the same level as the entering trains. Its Streamline Moderne design is more reminiscent of

18

Présence féminine by Gerald Gladstone

19

Katz's Delicatessen

20

Central Station

a ship than a train! The work *Monumental Frieze* by **Charles Comfort**, featured at opposite ends of the station, depicts, on the East wall, life in Canada, its national resources and industries, and on the West wall, leisure pursuits and fundamental freedoms. Underneath are French and English extracts from *O Canada*, composed by **Calixa Lavallée** and **Basile Routhier**, which was performed for the first time on June 24, 1880, but only officially became the Canadian national anthem a century later.

It is in this symbolic place that our first tour comes to an end. From here, you have the choice either to explore the streets of the downtown area outside, or to take the nearby metro to another destination. In fact, it's in the metro that our second circuit begins. To get there, head in the direction of Bonaventure metro station. At the end of a long corridor, go through the glass doors leading to the underground passageway via one of the two escalators, and follow the signs to the station.

PLACE VILLE MARIE

19

18

René-Lévesque

20 CENTRAL STATION

De la Gauchetière

PLACE BONAVENTURE

**TOUR 2
INTERNATIONAL
QUARTER: EXPLORING
MONTRÉAL'S
CORRIDORS OF
DESIGN**

START
Metro: Bonaventure, main plaza

END
Metro: Place-d'Armes, Place Jean-Paul-Riopelle square

REFERENCE POINTS

ARCHITECTURE
World Trade Centre Montréal

ART
Place Jean-Paul-Riopelle square

ENTERTAINMENT
Skating rink at 1000 De La Gauchetière

RESTAURANT
Osco! – InterContinental Hotel

Cathédrale

Mansfield

Bonaventure

2

1000 DE LA GAUCHETIÈRE

Saint-Antoine West

This walk takes us on an east-west trail through the indoor city, a more recent, artistic and design-influenced route. I find these simpler spaces with their varying atmospheres a refreshing change after the ultra-commercial down-town sector. Here you can hear the silence, clear your thoughts, and rest your eyes!

The International Quarter is the result of an ambitious revitalization project which began in 1999 and has since been awarded over thirty prizes and international distinctions. It is the showcase of a contemporary and forward-looking Montréal.

Off we go!

Our starting point is the main plaza of the metro's Mezzanine level, near the information panels.

■ Bonaventure station

1

Bonaventure station

This busy station is at the nerve centre of the commuter network. It has no integral works of art but can be considered a work in itself, with its **huge proportions** and **deep vaults**. Our tour begins in the direction of 1000 De La Gauchetière, but if you like, you

can also go the opposite way to explore nearby Windsor Station and the Bell Centre.

Go up two escalators in succession to come out of the metro station.

■ 1000 De La Gauchetière

As you come through the revolving doors, you'll immediately see the main attraction of this building: **Atrium Le 1000**, a **large indoor skating rink** open year round. Watching the skaters of all ages and abilities can be just as entertaining as actually skating oneself!

Turn left after the doors, then left again into the corridor leading towards Place Bonaventure and De La Gauchetière Street, to reach the building's main entrance. On the way you'll pass **Fusion**, selling artisan ice cream. Go on—treat yourself!

2

door skating rink n the 1000 De La Gauchetière

3 Tunnel Bonaventure

4 Fusion

5 Arrêt sur image by Stéphane Pratte

In the glass lobby of this postmodern construction built in 1992, admire the kinetic work *Arrêt sur image* ("Freeze frame") by **Stéphane Pratte**, which catches the light so effectively.

Take the central staircase up to the Mezzanine to get a better view of the back of the **Cathedral-Basilica of Mary, Queen of the World**, a scale replica of Saint Peter's Basilica in Rome and the seat of the Catholic archdiocese of Montréal. You'll see that these window panes were specially designed to frame the view of the cathedral dome.

Head back down and to the right, towards the side door marked "Tunnel Bonaventure." After going down an escalator, go through the door on the right towards Place Bonaventure. Walk to the next intersection and turn right, then left. There, an escalator will take you up to a huge exhibition hall.

■ **Place Bonaventure and Hilton Montréal Bonaventure Hotel**

Head towards the main entrance, near the information desk.

6

Underground Montréal

6
View or the back of the Cathedral-Basilica of Mary, Queen of the World

7
Exhibition hall of Place Bonaventure

7

The **ribbed concrete walls** are typical of the Brutalist architecture of the 1960s. This whole complex is built above the city centre's railway tracks. When it was opened in 1967, it was the largest commercial building in the world, with a bigger surface area than the Empire State Building! Over a million visitors attend its numerous trade shows and exhibitions every year.

Now follow me to one of my favourite secret hideaways, the **rooftop gardens of the Hilton Montréal Bonaventure Hotel**. Take the corridor to the right of the information desk, then follow the signs to the elevator: the reception is on the 8th floor (the only other floor open to the public). When you arrive, walk over to the large window that offers a panoramic view over the

centre and south west of the city, the 1000 De La Gauchetière building, the **Mary, Queen of the World cathedral**, and the **St. Lawrence River** over to the left in the distance. If you turn back towards the hotel reception, you'll also see rustic gardens, complete with a stream, and Montréal's first **heated outdoor swimming pool**
—an absolute delight during the winter! Don't hesitate to go outside; they have ducks that live here all year round, and a herb garden tended by the chef. I'm sure you'll appreciate this complete change of scenery; just don't tell anyone else about it!

Retrace your steps back down to the Place Bonaventure information desk, and from there follow the main corridor, on the right,

9

Marcello's

10

University Street

towards the **Place de la Cité Internationale**. On the way, you'll see some of the renovations carried out since 1998, including new **pink-coloured luminous panels**, and you'll pass **Marcello's**, an attractive market and deli, open only on weekdays.

At the end of the corridor, head up the stairs and towards the large windows that give a nice **view onto University Street**—one of the major arteries leading into town—and from where several of the buildings of the International Quarter are visible. Notice the steep gradient over 45 metres and the **colonnade representing the flags of the world**—22 pillars of differing sizes but all at the same height—revealing the existence of plateaus. In the winter, the sidewalks in front of these buildings are heated, which makes them much less hazardous! The use of **tandem street lighting** designed by **Michel Dallaire** was chosen here, as it cleverly reduces light pollution.

Continue by taking the nearest staircase on the left, the one with low steps, followed by another flight of stairs towards the Place de la Cité Internationale, which brings you to the **tunnel under University Street**.

This somewhat surgical-looking corridor belongs to the International Civil Aviation Organization (ICAO), who allow the public to use it but are cautious about security and prefer people not to linger. Nevertheless, once a year, it's transformed into an exhibit space for the **Nuit Blanche** all-nighter

9

10

11

event during the **Montréal en lumière** (High Lights) winter festival. At the end of the tunnel, two escalators will take you up to the surface.

■ **International Civil Aviation Organization (ICAO)**

When you go through the doors, you'll find yourself in an **immense hall** looking out over flags—including that of the UN, a reminder of the district's international character—and the **Stock Exchange Tower**, a plain dark-brown building with concrete corners, built in 1965 and home to the derivatives exchange and the headquarters of the International Air Transportation Association (IATA)*.

Make your way to the end of the hall, then take the stairs down into the glazed lobby that leads directly out onto Victoria Square, to reach the corridor leading to the Square-Victoria metro station. At the end of the corridor, take the metro exit on your right. Look around—you could be forgiven for thinking you're in Paris!

11
Stairs

12
Tunnel

13
Hall of the ICAO

14
Stock Exchange Tower

✳ Zoological note

With a bit of luck, you might see, on the 32nd floor of the Stock Exchange Tower, a couple of peregrine falcons. These medium-sized birds of prey, which have the fastest high-speed dive in the world, feed on other birds and small land animals. They make their home on the top of high buildings, but do not build nests as such.

13

14

■ Victoria Square

The Square-Victoria **metro entrance by Hector Guimard** is the only one of its kind outside Paris. It was made in 1900 in the Art Nouveau style and donated to the city of Montréal to commemorate the inauguration of its metro system in 1966. Rumour has it that the Paris authorities later attempted to recover it, as they had none in such good condition. But the "permanent loan" was made official in 2003, and in exchange, in 2011, the Montréal transit authority gifted the Paris metro with a very different piece of artwork: a mural depicting a pair of woman's lips, entitled *La Voix lactée*, by photographer Geneviève Cadieux. Anyhow, to come back to our surroundings . . . Admire the characteristic **white tiles** with **blue frieze** decorating the walls of the station exit, the staircase reproduced to exactly the same dimensions, the **cast-iron railings** with their plant- and snake-like forms, the overhead **"Metropolitain" sign**, the **globular lamp posts**, and the **three globe lights** over the flight of steps.

15

Metro entrance by Hector Guimard

16

Statue of Queen Victoria

The square itself stands on a reclaimed swamp and has had various uses in the past. Originally a hay market, it was also a site commemorating the dismantling of the fortifications, and in 1860 it was renamed in honour of Queen Victoria on the occasion of a visit by the then Prince of Wales to inaugurate the Victoria Bridge. In 1872, Lord Dufferin unveiled a **statue of the Queen** in the square; rumour had it that it was his (prettier) sister who had been the model. For the square's recent redevelopment, several trees were planted and modern terraces with sculptures, water jets, and **benches designed by Michel**

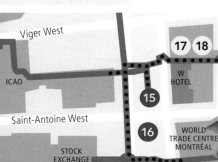

Viger West

ICAO

17 18

W HOTEL

15

Saint-Antoine West

16

WORLD TRADE CENTRE MONTRÉAL

STOCK EXCHANGE TOWER

16

17

**Entrance of
W Hotel**

18

*Stratifications
pariétales* by
Montréal artist
Christian Kiopini

Dallaire were added. On the other side of the street, notice the **blue entrance of the W Hotel**, as well as the coats of arms of the Canadian provinces in the centre of the lower windows, a reminder that this building formerly housed the **Canadian federal bank**.

Make your way back underground and take the white passageway on the right; we're going on a short detour.

■ **Tunnel under the W Hotel**

This elegant passageway has shiny, brightly lit walls and touches of blue, the colour of the W Hotel that sits above it. At the end you can see parts of the walls of the former bank vault. Along the way, you'll find *Stratifications pariétales* ("Wall stratifications")(2002-2003) by Montréal artist **Christian Kiopini**, a three-part geometrical work based on themes of geological formations and the former, underground purpose of this site. The earth's strata and its time periods are paradoxically represented by the colour blue of the river.

Turn back the way you came, heading towards Square-Victoria metro by going down an escalator,

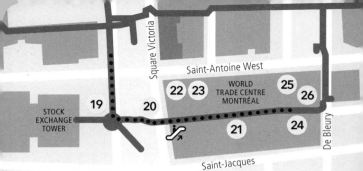

then turn left and follow signs for the World Trade Centre Montréal. You will come out into a rotunda.

■ Rotunda

The **Square-Victoria station rotunda** is a well-known meeting point with a surprising echo effect. Stand on the **black diamond** in the middle and exercise your voice. See what I mean? I always take the chance to sing a favourite tune or two!

From here, take the exit marked "Centre de commerce mondial" (World Trade Centre) via a **winding brick corridor**; the shapes, colours, and positions of the bricks have been varied to create texture. Going through the doors at the end, go up the escalator, which will bring you into a spectacular atrium.

19

Square-Victoria station rotunda

20

Winding brick corridor

21

World Trade Centre Montréal

■ **World Trade Centre Montréal**

Our very own World Trade Center, the **World Trade Centre Montréal**, is an office complex running the length of the former **Ruelle des Fortifications** (Fortification Lane)✶. Restoration work was carried out in the early 1990s to preserve the facades and historic character of the original buildings, and the whole was linked with a modern glass canopy. The complex contains several architectural treasures, including:

• a **new grey stone building** built in the heritage style and home to **Power Corporation**, the empire founded by the late **Paul Desmarais**;

• a huge **black granite pool** that sends back a perfect reflection

 Historical note

Fortification Lane stands on the site of the northern ramparts of the fortified city of Montréal, which were completed in 1730 but razed between 1804 and 1812 due to the city's rapid expansion. A hundred years ago, the lane was the service road for the big banks and insurance companies on Saint-Jacques Street.

from the still, smooth surface of its water, as fragile, one might say, as the financial world around it;

- stately **lamp posts** adorning the square;

- a **fountain decorated with an elegant statue of Amphitrite**, wife of Poseidon, by the French sculptor **Dieudonné-Barthélemy Guibal**, which was acquired by Paul Desmarais from an antique dealer in France.

Go up the steps behind the statue and cross the first footbridge on the right. At the end, take the walkway immediately to your left, which leads to the entrance of the ultra-chic **XO restaurant of the St. James Hotel**. The painted murals here remind us that this building once housed the reputable Nordheimer Piano Company.

Now take the next footbridge to reach the lobby of the **InterContinental Hotel**. In here are two epicurean gems: **Osco!**, a Provencal brasserie run by chef **Matthieu Saunier**, who makes delicious baguette and tapenade among many other mouth-watering delights, and **Sarah B.**, a unique and atmospheric absinthe bar.

22

Black granite pool

23

Statue of Amphitrite by French sculptor Dieudonné-Barthélemy Guibal

24
XO restaurant of the Saint-James Hotel

Head out of the lobby and down the escalator. "What's that covering the walls?" you might ask. Well, if you look more closely, you'll see that it's **mink fur** and birch bark—eye-catching and unconventional, to say the least!

At the bottom of the escalator, turn left and go through one of the doors in front of you to re-enter the main atrium. Nearby, a few steps to the right, is a **segment of the Berlin Wall**, a gift to the city of Montréal in 1992 for its 350th anniversary, with historical explanations provided on panels alongside it.

Turn back and continue towards the staircase at the very end of the complex, where, below the **glass roof pitched at 45°**, you'll discover the work *Circulations* (2012) by

25
Mink fur and birch bark covered wall

26
Segment of the Berlin Wall

Rafael Sottolichio, a colourful mural celebrating the 20th anniversary of the Trade Centre.

Take the door through to a space dedicated to the **Pointe-à-Callière Museum of Archeology and History**. Stop a moment to admire the mural, *Sous la ville d'aujourd'hui se cache un Montréal souterrain où se côtoient l'ancien et le nouveau* ("Under our city lies an underground Montréal where old meets new") (2003), which illustrates the hidden canals and rivers running under the city that have now mostly become passageways!

Go through the door just opposite, which takes you into a corridor leading towards the Palais des Congrès. Displayed along the corridor, in succession, are a

27

Circulations by **Rafael Sottolichio**

28

Tables by **Michel Goulet**

29

Le Grand Jean-Paul by **Roseline Granet**

(28)

(29)

photographic work entitled *Sleep (or periods underground)* (2005-2006), by **Isabelle Hayeur**, which reflects on consumption and the environment; a diptych, *Tables* (2005), by **Michel Goulet**, composed of two panels engraved with flags and universal pictograms symbolizing the international character of the area; and one of Goulet's famous chairs, a fine example of symbolic and functional art, albeit a little uncomfortable! This work also makes an amusing riddle that I play with my groups of visitors!

Go up the staircase opposite, which takes you out towards **Place Jean-Paul-Riopelle**, a public square built on top of the covered portion of the Ville-Marie expressway.

■ **Place Jean-Paul-Riopelle**

Your eye will be drawn to the life-size bronze of Jean-Paul Riopelle, *Le Grand Jean-Paul* ("The great Jean-Paul") (2003), by **Roseline Granet**. At the other end of the park is Riopelle's *La Joute* ("The joust") (1969), a fountain with twelve sculptures paying tribute to nature and the First Nations and

Underground Montréal

41

 Biographical note

Jean-Paul Riopelle was born in Montréal and became a world-renowned artist. In the 1940s, he studied at Montréal's school of furniture design, where he met Paul-Émile Borduas. In 1948, he signed the *Refus global* anti-establishment manifesto with 14 other abstract painters from Québec. After World War II, he settled in France, where he befriended André Breton, Alberto Giacometti, and Samuel Beckett. He returned to Québec in the early 1990s and died in 2002 at his home in Isle-aux-Grues.

depicting figures of humans, bears, dogs, and owls. During the summer, the composition is brought to life with a water and lighting display.

You'll also notice the elegant **CDP Capital Centre**, home to the Montréal offices of the Caisse de dépôt et placement du Québec. The building has received several awards and is filled with innovative features. One of its prides is the haute-cuisine restaurant **Toqué!**, owned and run by chef **Normand Laprise**, who has led the way in promoting Québec cuisine and local produce.

On the other side of the square stands the **coloured glass façade of the Palais des Congrès**, designed by architect **Mario Saia** and his team. In the upper left corner is the outer panel of the diptych *Translucide* (2003), a collective work representing a face and hand touching through the interplay of light and shadow, and said to be the **largest contemporary figurative work of stained glass** in America at the time of its installation.

This anthology of art brings us to the end of our tour through

30

Coloured glass façade of the Palais des Congrès

31
Corridor of contrasting yellow and black

the international sector of underground Montréal, a labyrinth of passages with particularly esthetic appeal. The district's developers have succeeded in creating an image of a sophisticated and contemporary city.

If you like, you can now cross the street to 1001 **Place Jean-Paul-Riopelle** and enter the Hall Place Riopelle—the main lobby of the Palais des Congrès—where our third tour begins. Or, if you prefer to take the indoor route, head back down to the corridor where we saw the works by Goulet and keep going straight on until it joins up with the passageway under the CDP Capital Centre, which you'll take to the right. At the end, turn left into a corridor of contrasting yellow and black, and travel up the escalator to your left. You'll come out at the Palais des Congrès, from where you can reach the Place Riopelle lobby just next to it.

■ **Palais des Congrès**

From this point, follow the main corridor to the end to reach the **Place-d'Armes metro** station; you'll see several signs. You might also want to go out of the station to explore nearby **Chinatown** or **Old Montréal**.

**TOUR 3
ENTERTAINMENT
DISTRICT: FOOTSTEPS
TOWARDS CULTURAL
MONTRÉAL**

START
Metro: Place-d'Armes,
1001 Place Jean-Paul-Riopelle
– Palais des Congrès

END
Metro: Place-des-Arts,
Place des Festivals

REFERENCE POINTS

ARCHITECTURE
Atrium – Complexe
Desjardins

ART
Foyer – Place des Arts

Espace culturel
Georges-Émile-Lapalme

ENTERTAINMENT
Museum of Contemporary
Art

RESTAURANT
Place Deschamps – Place des
Arts

In this walk we'll explore the secondary north-south section of the RÉSO, which takes us into the heart of Montréal's cultural life. These corridors might seem less impressive than those of the International Quarter, but the abundance of light and large open spaces transform this area of the indoor city into something that no longer feels underground. This visit will convince you that the "below-ground Montréal" really is an exceptional accomplishment.

■ Palais des Congrès

Our tour begins in the west lobby of the Palais des Congrès, a conference and exhibition centre constructed over the Ville-Marie expressway on the site of a building dating from the 1970s.

Viger West

PALAIS DES CONGRÈS

Saint-Antoine West

1

he Constellation of
Great Montrealers

Inaugurated in May 1983, it under-
went major expansion and renovation work in the early 2000s to
double its capacity. Today it is one
of the busiest convention centres
in North America, hosting numerous international congresses each
year.

In the **Hall Place Riopelle** lobby,
along Saint-Antoine Street, you'll
see a **large blue mural**, entitled
*The Constellation of Great
Montrealers* (2012), which pays
tribute to over a hundred people
who have helped shape the city.
Each one is represented by a
dot of light (a star) and a symbol
indicating the field in which they
contributed (cultural, economic,
scientific, social, etc.). See if you
can find the names of some great
Montrealers you know.

Underground Montréal

2
Lipstick Forest by
Claude Cormier

3
Noobox

Near this hall, you won't be able to miss the highly original *Lipstick Forest* (2002) by **Claude Cormier**, featuring 52 bright pink concrete tree trunks modelled on the hundred-year-old trees lining Montréal's Park Avenue. The lipstick pink celebrates the local cosmetics industry that inspired the colour and symbolizes the joie de vivre so characteristic of the city.

Walk down the wide corridor, where you'll find shops and take-out food counters, including **Noobox**, which offers a simple and affordable concept of fresh Asian food presented in a distinctive box. Head to the entrance of the Place-d'Armes metro station by following the signs leading to **Hall Viger**. This is one of the shallower stations in Montréal, as it is built

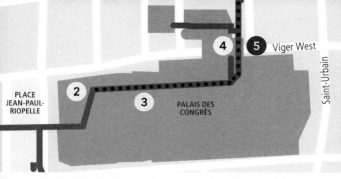

PLACE
JEAN-PAUL-
RIOPELLE

2

3

4

5 Viger West

Saint-Urbain

PALAIS DES
CONGRÈS

4

**Footbridge
overlooking Viger
Avenue**

on the former site of the St. Martin River, which has today been channelized. Nearby, go up the escalator leading to a footbridge and follow signs to Complexe Guy-Favreau.

■ **Footbridge overlooking Viger Avenue: views of Old Montréal and Chinatown**

At this point, underground Montréal becomes overground Montréal. Stop to take in the views of the area around Viger Avenue, which is named after the city's first mayor, Jacques Viger (1833-1836). To your right, you will see:

• the handsome **Jacques-Cartier Bridge**, opened in 1930 and originally named the Montreal Harbour Bridge;

4

- the clock sign on the **Molson Brewery**, a city landmark and a thriving Québec business;

- the light-grey tower of the new **Montréal university hospital centre** (CHUM);

- the Feng Shui-inspired yellow bricks, corner front entrance, and pagoda-style roof of the **Holiday Inn Hotel**, Chinatown;

- the octagonal windows of the **Saint-Esprit Chinese Catholic Mission community centre**, where the Chinese language and tai chi are taught.

From here, you have the choice either to continue inside to the Guy-Favreau Complex, or to step outside for a few minutes to dis-cover a charming little square in **Chinatown**.

If you choose the fresh air option, take the exit on your left, which comes out behind the Guy-Favreau Complex. Otherwise, just skip the following directions.

■ **Small square, Palais des Congrès**

On this little trip outside you'll discover a very pleasant urban space. On your left, the grey stone **Church of the Saint-Esprit Chinese Catholic Mission** (1834-1835) is one of the oldest places of worship still standing in Montréal and has had a string of owners—Scottish, French, Slovakian, Chinese, and others.

On the other side of the square is the **Wing house** (1826), the oldest building in the district, which was

6

Wing house

built by Scottish entrepreneur **John Redpath** and became a noodle and fortune cookie factory in 1910. No doubt the creator of the first **bilingual fortune cookies**, **Arthur Lee**, made his fortune from them! Go to 1009 Côté Street to sample some and find out what your future holds. I can assure you that the messages are always positive—though not always comprehensible!

■ **Guy-Favreau Complex**

As you come into this complex and make your way along the **corridor with skylights**, it's immediately clear from the security guards on duty that this is a government building. Elderly members of the Chinese community come to chat on the benches here. Just before the end of the corridor, take the first escalator up to ground level, where you'll see a **pretty outdoor courtyard** with several species of trees, including some beautiful **Ginkgo biloba** (Maidenhair).

Walk around the vast **atrium of the Guy-Favreau Complex** to the stairs on the other side. The building you are in was built in 1984—after much procrastination by the Canadian government—on

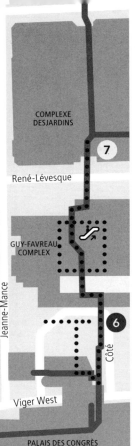

the former Dufferin Square, which was a meeting place for the Jewish community and itself on the site of a Protestant cemetery (1799-1847). The building has huge multistoried windows and was designed to provide an unobstructed view from the **Place des Arts** to **Place d'Armes**. One might easily imagine the rivalry with its neighbouring complex, which has similarly vast expanses of glass. In the main entrance stands a **bronze bust of Guy Favreau**, Canadian politician and judge, bearing the quote: "Tolerance is the condition of the dignity of men as well as their cultures"—still true today★!

Go down to the tunnel passing under René-Lévesque Boulevard and leading to Complexe Desjardins, which you will come into via two escalators (or an elevator).

■ Complexe Desjardins

On the right as you enter the complex you'll find the **Coordonnerie Desjardins** shoe repair shop, complete with traditional shoe-shine service. If you chat to the friendly owner, he'll be pleased to tell you more about this disappearing craft.

 **Anecdote**

The multifunctional Guy-Favreau Complex, built hastily with inferior quality materials, began to crumble quite seriously just four years after its construction. The Chinese elders were said to have taken this as a sign of disapproval by their ancestors' spirits that the building was erected on former burial ground.

Now go up the escalator to the **Grande-Place**, a central plaza surrounded by shops on two floors. Built in 1967 after the Quiet Revolution and located in a traditionally French-speaking part of the city, Complexe Desjardins symbolizes the rise of French-Canadians in America. It houses the administrative headquarters of a financial cooperative founded by **Alphonse and Dorimène Desjardins** in 1900. At the time of its inauguration, the octagonal shape of its towers was unique in North America. The building's design, with its **two immense glass windows** that flood the space with natural light, reflects the wish of former Mayor Jean Drapeau that someone standing in

Underground Montréal

7

Shoe-shine service of Coordonnerie Desjardins

7

8

the middle of the complex should be able to see both the Place des Arts and the bell towers of the Notre-Dame Basilica. Since then, however, the construction of the Palais des Congrès has obstructed part of this view.

The focal point of this plaza is the fountain, *Kynégraph* (2012), by **Olivier Dufour**, a world-renowned Québec artist, and a collective of over 200 other artists. Take in the spectacle of its beautiful water displays. During Holiday season, this area is filled with decorations, and families flock to meet Santa—the *real* **Santa Claus**, of course!

Browse the various stores, treat yourself to something sweet, or perhaps buy yourself a book . . . there's something here for

8

everyone. I suggest **La boulange-rie moderne**, offering tempting fresh-baked fare, and **L'Art des artisans du Québec**, a shop selling original creations from more than 150 local artists.

If you happen to be here at aperitif time, go up to the 6th floor to the **Hyatt Regency Hotel cocktail lounge**, a very pleasant and afford-able spot that not many people know about. In the summer, enjoy a drink outside on the hotel's roof terrace.

Continue on to the passageway under Sainte-Catherine Street, following signs to Place-des-Arts metro station.

■ **Place des Arts**

At the end of the tunnel, take the escalator up to the main floor.

In this foyer, you'll find **Place Deschamps**, a wine bar named after the hugely popular Québec comedian **Yvon Deschamps**, who regularly performs at the Place des Arts. This is a great spot for a drink and a bite to eat with friends just before a show. Right next to it is *Comme si le temps... de la rue* ("As if time… from the street") (1992), by **Pierre Granche**, a work in the semicircular form of a Greek theatre and representing the city's urban fabric from the St. Lawrence River to Mount Royal, with white sculptured aluminium figures resembling totem poles or caryatids.

A little further on, you'll come to the entrance of the Museum of Contemporary Art and its gift

55

Underground Montréal

shop, directly connected to the indoor network. Both are well worth a look around. The shop sells a wide range of original creations, and the museum is quite simply amazing!

■ Montréal Museum of Contemporary Art

Established in 1964, this was the first museum in Canada dedicated entirely to contemporary works produced after 1939 from Québec and around the world. Its permanent collection includes the largest collection of art by **Paul-Émile Borduas**. The esthetically pleasing interior is laid out around an impressive **circular hall**.

Take your time to look around, before retracing your steps.

■ Place des Arts

If this performing arts centre exists, it's thanks to the persistence of a group of influential supporters of **Mayor Jean Drapeau** (yes, him again!) intent on equipping Montréal with modern cultural infrastructure of international calibre. Work began in 1961, and the main performance hall was inaugurated in September 1963,

9

Comme si le temps... de la rue by Pierre Granche

9

10

Entrance of the Montréal Museum of Contemporary Art

with a concert conducted by **Wilfrid Pelletier**, in whose honour the same hall was renamed in 1966. Claude Léveillée was the first Québec artist to perform a show here. This stage is also home to **Les Grands Ballets Canadiens** and the **Opéra de Montréal**. The many works of art include *Amor*, eight ceramic high-reliefs by **Jordi Bonet** symbolizing love and fertility, which sit above the doors leading into the hall. You can also see tapestries by artists **Micheline Beauchemin** and **Robert Lapalme**. Finally, if you have the chance to stay for a show, do take a look around the galleries and foyers surrounding the auditorium.

Continue your walk by returning to the main central walkway, the Espace Culturel Georges-Émile-Lapalme, where various live performances take place regularly. In this area you can also visit the Exhibition Room, where a variety of free events on the performing arts theme are held throughout the year, and try out the amusing interactive multimedia wall.

11
Glass ceiling by Claude Bettinger

12
Salon urbain

In the centre of this space, admire *Glass Ceiling* (1992) by **Claude Bettinger**, a work resembling a telescope, kaleidoscope and periscope all in one, with an angel pointing to the sky. This unique skylight is visible from above ground as well as below, and reminds us that "The artist is one who makes you see the other side of things"; in fact, the original French statement is etched somewhere in the work—see if you can spot it! From outside you can get a better overall view of the work; just take one of the side doors out onto the **Place des Arts esplanade**. From here you have an impressive view of Complexe Desjardins, **Théâtre Maisonneuve**, **Salle Wilfrid-Pelletier**, the **Maison Symphonique** concert hall, and the **Museum of Contemporary Art**. Also admire the landscaping, **lamp posts**, and other typical features of this space.

Go back inside through the same door you came out of, and follow signs for Saint-Urbain Street. Along the way you'll pass the **Salon urbain**, a trendy meeting space concealed behind translucent red curtains—not unlike a

11

11

giant piece of origami! On from here are the **ARTV Studio** and the **Maison symphonique de Montréal**, the youngest of the city's concert halls, inaugurated in September 2011, where the Montréal Symphony Orchestra (OSM), the Orchestre métropolitain, I Musici de Montréal, Les Violons du Roy, and other classical music ensembles perform. OSM music director **Kent Nagano** has said that the venue has the best acoustics for orchestral music in the world. Its **pipe organ**, made by the prestigious Casavant Frères in Saint-Hyacinthe, has 109 registers, 83 stops, 116 ranks and 6,489 pipes.

12

SALON URBAIN

De Maisonneuve

Place-des-Arts

SALLE WILFRID-PELLETIER

MAISON SYMPHONIQUE

15

14

13

Jeanne-Mance

Saint-Urbain

MONTRÉAL MUSEUM OF CONTEMPORARY ART

PLACE DES ARTS ESPLANADE

THÉÂTRE MAISONNEUVE

13

Salle Wilfrid-Pelletier of Place-des-Arts

14

La Cinquième salle of Place-des-Arts

Make your way back towards the Cinquième Salle concert hall and the Place-des-Arts metro. You'll pass **Le Seingalt** restaurant, which displays **costumes from productions** put on at the Place des Arts, and a branch of the music and book store **Archambault**, a Québec business founded in 1896 that started out selling sheet music. Check out the posters advertising upcoming shows and performances.

Go through two series of doors taking you into the metro station.

■ **Place-des-Arts station**

Immediately on entering you'll see an immense **backlit stained-glass** mural protected by steel supports and shimmering with vibrant

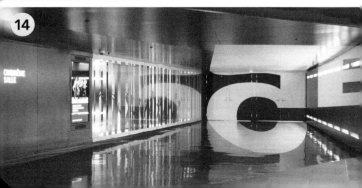

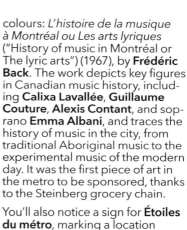

colours: *L'histoire de la musique à Montréal ou Les arts lyriques* ("History of music in Montréal or The lyric arts") (1967), by **Frédéric Back**. The work depicts key figures in Canadian music history, including **Calixa Lavallée**, **Guillaume Couture**, **Alexis Contant**, and soprano **Emma Albani**, and traces the history of music in the city, from traditional Aboriginal music to the experimental music of the modern day. It was the first piece of art in the metro to be sponsored, thanks to the Steinberg grocery chain.

You'll also notice a sign for **Étoiles du métro**, marking a location where the best street musicians, specially chosen by Montréal's transit authority, can perform. Pause to appreciate and encourage their talent, which they enjoy sharing with passers-by. Music is omnipresent in the Montréal metro, and buskers are allowed anywhere you see a sign **depicting a lyre**. Their music provides gaiety and conviviality, especially at rush hour, for our listening pleasure!

Now take the escalator to the left of the turnstiles, which comes out at the **Place des Festivals**, our final destination.

15

L'histoire de la musique à Montréal ou Les arts lyriques by Frédéric Back

15

Place-des-Arts

SALLE
WILFRID-
PELLETIER

MAISON
SYMPHONIQUE

PLACE
DES
FESTIVALS

Jeanne-Mance

De Bleury

Saint-Urbain

MONTRÉAL
MUSEUM OF
CONTEMPORARY
ART

PLACE
DES ARTS
ESPLANADE

THÉÂTRE
MAISONNEUVE

Sainte-Catherine

■ Place des Festivals, Quartier des Spectacles

As soon as you exit the metro, you'll see the Place des Festivals. This public square within the Quartier des spectacles (the entertainment district) was inaugurated in September 2009 and runs along Jeanne-Mance Street opposite the contemporary art museum. It features **235 hi-tech water jets** that light up in red and white at night and which, like in all big cities, offer cool respite and fun for kids during hot summer days. This is the outdoor venue for all of Montréal's major festivals: the **International Jazz Festival**, **FrancoFolies**, **Just for Laughs**, **Montréal High Lights Festival**, and so on. The square's appearance changes with the seasons, including interactive installations every winter.

Stop awhile to soak up the atmosphere of this space—which showcases the best of Montréal culture and of which the city is extremely proud—before heading off towards new adventures.

We've reached the end of our excursion through the underground city and the stories it has to tell. I recommend you explore these corridors regularly, if you can, because their atmospheres change according to the time of day, the season, and the many events held in the city throughout the year.

CONCLUSION

Underground Montréal is a multi-faceted place, a fascinating mix of shadow and daylight. In the decades to come, this indoor network will inevitably expand to connect new areas of the city, reaching new and up-and-coming neighbourhoods such as the Quartier de la santé (health district), Quartier de l'innovation (innovation district), Cité du multimédia, and Griffintown, thus creating opportunities for new circuits and discoveries. You can follow developments on the website of the Université de Montréal's indoor city observatory, at: www.observatoiredelavilleinterieure.ca/.

Now that you've learned more about these hidden routes through Montréal and captured their essence, I'm sure you'll want to see what other surprises they have in store. Do keep me posted—tour guides love to receive feedback!

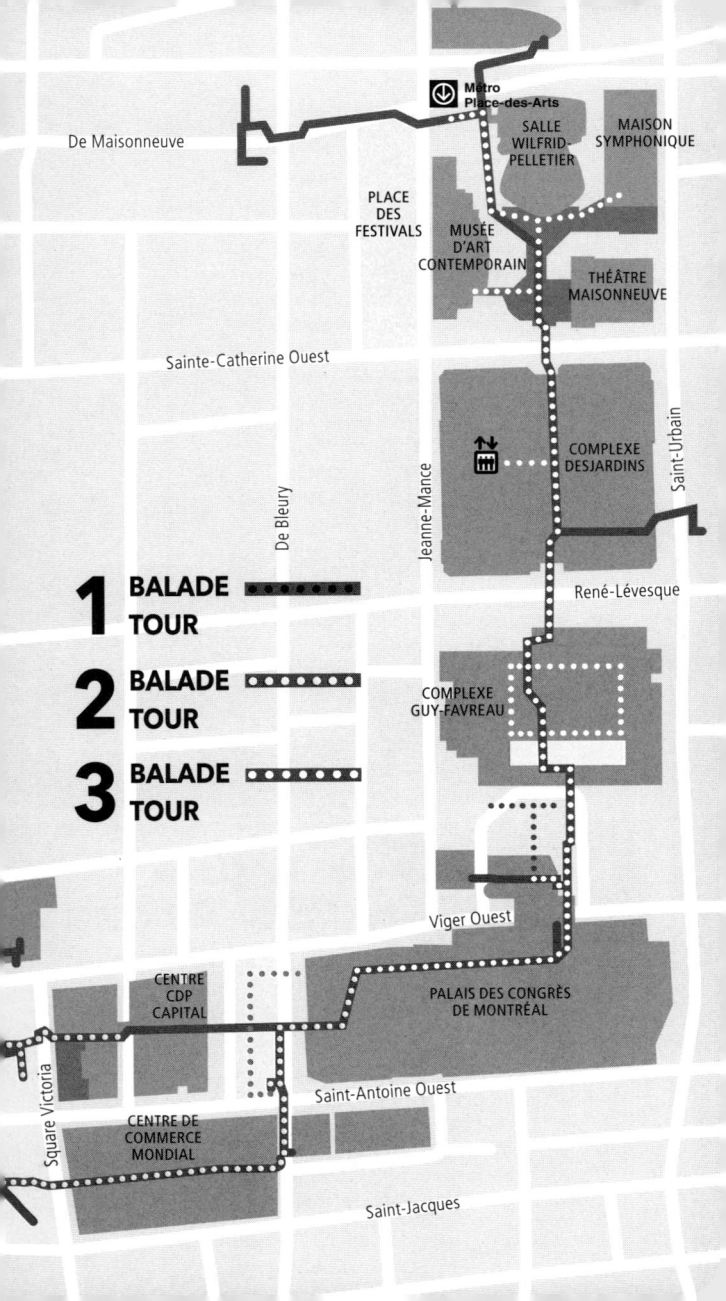

AVANT-PROPOS

INTRODUCTION

BALADE 1
Le centre-ville : marcher la genèse du Montréal marchand

BALADE 2
Le Quartier international : foulées dans les galeries du Montréal design

BALADE 3
Quartier des spectacles : à pas couverts vers le Montréal culturel

CONCLUSION

AVANT-PROPOS

Il faut avoir voyagé dans plusieurs pays et côtoyé des touristes à Montréal pour s'apercevoir à quel point la ville souterraine est un mystère pour plusieurs. On ne sait pas exactement ce qu'elle est ni où sont ses accès, et on s'y égare. Je vous propose ici quelques itinéraires que je réalise souvent avec des visiteurs en tant que guide accrédité de Montréal, et au fil desquels je vous dévoilerai avec plaisir ses petits secrets.

Beauceron d'origine, j'ai complété un baccalauréat en administration des affaires, option tourisme, à l'UQAM en 1977. J'ai ensuite parcouru le monde à titre de guide professionnel et d'explorateur pendant plus de quinze ans. J'ai enfin décidé de m'installer à Montréal, qui m'était alors méconnue, et de partir à sa découverte comme si j'étais dans une ville étrangère. Mes semelles ont foulé plusieurs fois les rues de tous ses quartiers. Je l'ai aimée sous toutes ses coutures, pour sa diversité,

ses ambiances et son histoire, ou plutôt *ses* histoires… J'ai voulu que les regards de tous pour elle soient aussi émerveillés et curieux que le mien, et trouver une façon de la découvrir par tous nos sens. J'aime faire luire ses attraits et apprécier ses quelques cicatrices.

C'est ainsi qu'est né Tours Kaléidoscope (www.tourskaleidoscope. com), pour permettre à tous de découvrir les quartiers, les différentes cultures et les richesses patrimoniales de Montréal. Je suis un fier ambassadeur de notre belle ville.

Alors, suivez le guide!

INTRODUCTION

Le réseau piétonnier intérieur de Montréal est le plus vaste et le plus diversifié du monde. Il attise la curiosité et fait la convoitise de plusieurs grandes villes. Comme tous les lieux familiers, ses usagers ne le remarquent toutefois plus. Mon défi est de vous faire découvrir les particularités de ces lieux uniques. S'y inscrivent les défis, les rêves d'avenir et l'audace des bâtisseurs et des habitants de Montréal.

Mais qu'est-ce, au juste, que cette ville souterraine ? Au sens strict, il ne s'agit pas d'un lieu où logent des gens; les Montréalais ne sont ni des taupes ni des personnages de science-fiction. Au contraire, ils adorent profiter de leur belle ville à ciel ouvert ! C'est plutôt un univers parallèle, un entrelacs de passages, de tunnels et d'espaces intérieurs permettant la circulation piétonnière entre le cœur de la ville et le Vieux-Montréal, et qui se développe en symbiose avec le métro*. Le segment le plus utilisé, qu'on a baptisé RÉSO*, est d'ailleurs

Enfin, le métro!

Au Québec, le développement d'un métro entièrement souterrain et roulant sur pneumatiques est lancé après la Révolution tranquille. En octobre 1966, 3 lignes et 20 stations sont inaugurées. Il compte aujourd'hui 4 lignes et 68 stations.

parfois signalé près des entrées extérieures du métro. Les usagers l'apprécient énormément, car il protège en toute saison des intempéries et des variations climatiques. J'adore déambuler en plein cœur de la ville en simples chaussures au mois de février!

Je vous propose trois balades sillonnant respectivement le centre-ville, le Quartier international et le Quartier des spectacles, d'une durée d'environ une à deux heures chacune selon votre rythme et vos arrêts. Elles peuvent être réalisées individuellement ou facilement enchaînées, et totalisent environ cinq kilomètres. Enfilez vos meilleures chaussures de marche et laissez-vous entraîner dans un safari urbain pour explorer les profondeurs de Montréal… sans vous y perdre!

Le RÉSO

Emprunté par plus de 500 000 usagers par jour, il réunit environ 32 kilomètres de couloirs piétonniers reliant plus de 200 points d'accès, 10 stations de métro, des gares de trains et d'autobus, une centaine d'immeubles et pavillons universitaires, et plus de 2000 commerces.

**BALADE 1
LE CENTRE-VILLE :
MARCHER LA GENÈSE
DU MONTRÉAL
MARCHAND**

DÉPART

Métro : station Peel, sortie
Peel Sud, vers les Cours
Mont-Royal

ARRIVÉE

Métro : station Bonaventure,
gare Centrale

REPÈRES

ARCHITECTURE
Atrium – complexe Les Ailes

ART
Solstice – Carrefour
Industrielle-Alliance

DIVERTISSEMENT
Musée Grévin – Centre Eaton

RESTAURANT
Katz's Delicatessen – place
Ville-Marie

(1)

1

Motifs sur céramique – 54 cercles de Jean-Paul Mousseau

Au cours de cette balade, je vous raconterai l'évolution de la ville intérieure imaginée par ses créateurs, soucieux d'un environnement convivial bénéficiant de la lumière naturelle afin que l'usager ne souffre pas de claustrophobie. Au fil de nos pas, vous comprendrez mieux la logique de son développement à partir du centre-ville.

■ Station Peel

Notre balade débute dans le métro sur un grand cercle de céramique colorée dont un carreau est signé. Vous marchez sur l'art! Il s'agit de l'œuvre *Motifs sur céramique – 54 cercles* (1964) de **Jean-Paul Mousseau**, élève de Paul-Émile Borduas. Les cercles, tous différents, sont répartis partout dans la station,

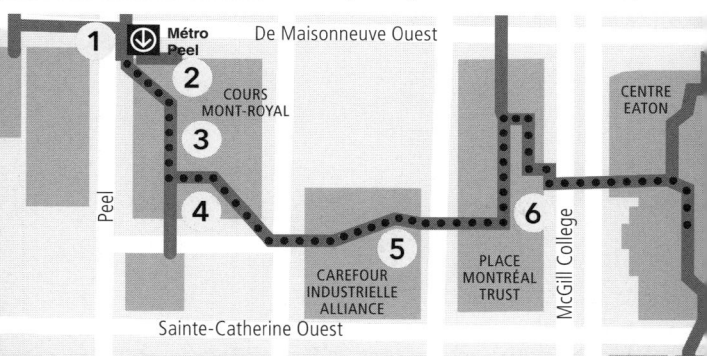

2

Grand escalier dans les Cours Mont-Royal

3

Cours Mont-Royal : jardins tropicaux

4

Cours Mont-Royal : lustre

2

Le Montréal souterrain

3

4

et l'un des grands cercles des quais est dédié à la conjointe de l'artiste. Si vous faites le compte, ne soyez pas surpris d'en trouver seulement 37, et non 54, certains ayant disparu lors de réaménagements.

Sortez du métro et suivez les indications en direction des Cours Mont-Royal.

■ **Cours Mont-Royal**

À l'entrée de la première cour, empruntez le grand escalier gris-vert à votre gauche. Devant se trouvent des **jardins tropicaux**, oasis inattendue qui vaut le détour. Accédez au second niveau par l'escalier mobile situé derrière l'escalier gris-vert que vous venez d'emprunter, puis tournez à droite. Levez les yeux et voyez, au-dessus de l'escalier, les **sculptures**

⭐ **Note historique**

Érigé en 1922, l'hôtel Mont-Royal de style Beaux-Arts
était rehaussé de touches néogéorgiennes et néoba-
roques. Comptant plus de mille chambres, il était alors le
plus vaste de l'Empire britannique, ce qui faisait dire que
l'on pouvait *y naître et mourir sans en sortir…*

5

Solstice du
**sculpteur Guido
Molinari**

6

**Le grand atrium
de la place
Montréal Trust**

suspendues d'hommes oiseaux,
ou *tingmiluks*, de David Ruben
Piqtoukun, artiste autochtone
reconnu. Ces sculptures repré-
sentent des chamans ailés dont
le vol est possible grâce à l'esprit
inuit maître du vent, Sila. Un peu
plus loin, au cœur de la voûte, se
trouve un **majestueux lustre** pro-
venant du casino de Monte-Carlo
qui rehausse la splendeur du lieu et
rappelle l'époque de l'hôtel Mont-
Royal⭐. Fermé en 1983, l'établissement a par la suite été converti
en centre d'affaires et en galeries
de boutiques de créateurs et de
marques internationales.

Continuez jusqu'au bout de la
galerie et tournez à gauche pour
emprunter un escalier mobile
puis un grand escalier gris afin de
redescendre au niveau Métro. Une
foire alimentaire s'étend alors droit
devant vous. Pour poursuivre la
balade, enfilez le passage Cours
Mont-Royal, à gauche, en direction
du Carrefour Industrielle-Alliance.

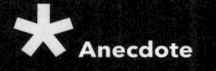

⭐ **Anecdote**

La prestigieuse avenue McGill College a failli être vendue
à un promoteur désireux de la couvrir d'une verrière pour
y installer des boutiques et une salle de concert. Le maire
Drapeau avait donné son aval à la transaction, mais la
population s'est mobilisée pour bloquer le projet.

■ Carrefour Industrielle-Alliance

Une fois dans le complexe, repérez l'entrée du magasin Simons et montez l'escalier mobile pour admirer au plafond l'œuvre astrologique *Solstice* (1999), tout en plexiglas, du sculpteur **Guido Molinari**, figure marquante de l'école géométrique abstraite de Montréal. Ce mobile géant aux couleurs vives symbolise le passage des saisons de la mode et a été mis en mouvement par le designer industriel **Michel Dallaire**.

Redescendez et continuez vers la place Montréal Trust, à droite.

■ Place Montréal Trust

Vous débouchez sur la galerie du **grand atrium** de style brutaliste, naturel et sans ornementation. Il est coiffé d'un toit de verre qui brise la sensation d'enfermement, et rehaussé en son centre de l'œuvre en cuivre *Fontaine intérieure* (1988) de **Zeidler Roberts**, qui s'enorgueillit de l'un des plus hauts jets d'eau intérieurs en Amérique du Nord. La fontaine se transforme en sapin multimédia interactif pendant la saison des fêtes hivernales.

Contournez l'atrium par la gauche pour rejoindre la galerie opposée, vers le kiosque d'information. En chemin, vous croiserez une succursale du magasin **Omer DeSerres**, une entreprise familiale de matériel d'artiste et de loisirs fondée en 1908. Empruntez ensuite le tunnel qui passe sous l'avenue McGill College en direction du Centre Eaton.

■ Centre Eaton[*]

Dirigez-vous vers la voûte et tournez à droite dans l'allée. Un ascenseur vitré vous attend quelques mètres plus loin. Empruntez-le jusqu'au 5ᵉ étage pour accéder au **musée Grévin Montréal**. Vous y trouverez plus d'une centaine de statues de cire de personnalités québécoises et internationales ayant marqué l'histoire, la culture ou l'actualité. Une expérience immersive et amusante, et de nombreuses photos cocasses à partager par la suite! Sur place, une boutique de souvenirs et le Café Grévin, signé **Jérôme Ferrer**, chef québécois de renom. Je vous recommande notamment son abordable boîte à lunch et ses délicieux macarons frais.

Avant de redescendre, prenez le temps d'apprécier la structure étagée ainsi que la splendide verrière de **Peter Rose**, pour laquelle il a reçu le prix d'excellence de l'Ordre des architectes du Québec en 1991. L'architecte montréalais a également conçu le Centre canadien d'architecture.

7
Café Grévin

8
Verrière
de Peter Rose

9
Murales de
Maurice Savoie

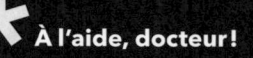

✱ À l'aide, docteur!

Le Centre Eaton, inauguré en 1976 et alors appelé Les Terrasses, avait été conçu d'après les savantes recommandations de psychologues de la consommation (*spin doctors*) afin de forcer les gens à circuler, et donc à consommer. Trop complexe, ce labyrinthe a toutefois été boudé par les clients! En 1986, l'endroit change de nom, revient graduellement à une organisation plus simple et se voit rénové selon les nouvelles tendances… décrétées par les experts

Reprenez l'ascenseur jusqu'au niveau Métro (2), rendez-vous de l'autre côté du centre, direction métro McGill, et entrez dans la station.

■ Station McGill

Allez jusqu'aux portes du complexe Les Ailes, à droite. Située au cœur du centre-ville, cette station achalandée dessert plusieurs commerces et bureaux ainsi que l'université éponyme. On y découvre quelques œuvres d'art, parmi lesquelles, de part et d'autre des portes du complexe, *Murales* (1966) de **Maurice Savoie**, à savoir de fins bas-reliefs en terre cuite représentant fleurs, feuilles et animaux.

Empruntez ensuite la traverse en face de l'entrée du complexe pour atteindre la galerie opposée de la station. Observez en contrebas – sur les quais – cinq verrières de verre peint signées **Nicolas Sollogoub**. *La vie à Montréal au XIXe siècle* (1964-1969) évoque des scènes montréalaises des années 1800 : la chapelle Notre-Dame-de-Bon-Secours ; le séminaire des Sulpiciens ; Jacques Viger et Peter McGill, maires de Montréal, et les anciennes armoiries de la ville ; le

Le Montréal souterrain

15

10

Exposition sur l'histoire de la cathédrale Christ Church

11

Buste de Raoul Wallenberg

12

Édifice KPMG

bateau à vapeur de John Molson et certaines activités économiques de l'époque.

Revenez sur vos pas vers l'entrée du complexe Les Ailes. Juste à gauche de l'entrée, vous trouverez la murale *C'est sur le sol qu'on prend appui pour s'envoler* (1991) du groupe artistique les **Industries perdues**, soit une maquette détaillée de l'île de Montréal en vue aérienne sous des blocs de verre. Prenez le temps de repérer les bâtiments que vous connaissez.

Continuez à longer la galerie jusqu'à l'entrée des Promenades Cathédrale, à droite.

■ **Promenades Cathédrale**

Passez les portes, tournez à gauche, puis à droite pour découvrir une exposition relatant l'étonnante histoire de la **cathédrale anglicane Christ Church**, joyau du patrimoine religieux de la plus ancienne paroisse anglophone de Montréal… et du centre commercial, un véritable temple marchand situé sous le lieu de culte* !

Poursuivez le long du corridor et tournez à droite au premier couloir jusqu'au carrefour suivant.

10

✱ Note historique

Construite en 1859 sur le modèle de celle de Salisbury en Angleterre, la cathédrale anglicane Christ Church a vite commencé à s'enfoncer vu un sol marécageux. Peu après son achèvement, le clocher en pierre est retiré pour limiter les dégâts et remplacé 15 ans plus tard par une réplique en aluminium. Depuis 1987, la cathédrale est soutenue par 21 profonds piliers et elle ne s'enfonce plus. Il y a des miracles techniques !

Vous pouvez ici aller mettre le nez dehors en montant l'escalier mobile à votre droite, lequel vous mènera derrière l'édifice KPMG dans une paisible cour intérieure, la **place Raoul Wallenberg**, dédiée à un diplomate qui a sauvé des milliers de Juifs pendant la Seconde Guerre mondiale. Admirez les verrières qui reprennent les formes d'ogives de la cathédrale.

Pour poursuivre la balade, continuez tout droit et entrez dans le complexe Les Ailes.

■ **Complexe Les Ailes**

Empruntez l'escalier mobile pour vous rendre au niveau Rez-de-chaussée. Aménagés en 1999, les **espaces intérieurs** et la **galerie à colonnade** du complexe Les Ailes sont grandioses, émulant les Galeries Lafayette à Paris, Macy's à New York et Harrods à Londres⋆. Malheureusement, la situation économique suivant les événements du 11 septembre 2001 n'a pas permis aux boutiques de luxe de prospérer. En 2007, le complexe a donc adopté une vocation commerciale plus modeste, et il abrite désormais des bureaux aux étages supérieurs.

✱ **Note historique**

Construit en 1925, l'édifice qu'occupe le complexe Les Ailes abritait à l'origine l'ancien Eaton, un grand magasin de détail, et le célèbre restaurant Le 9ᵉ, dont la salle à manger Art déco s'inspirait du paquebot *Île-de-France*. Cet espace a été conservé intact, mais il est inaccessible

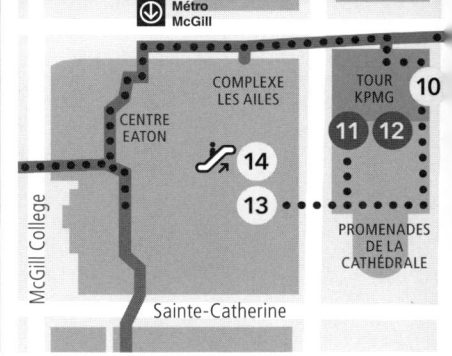

Métro
McGill

COMPLEXE
LES AILES

CENTRE
EATON

TOUR
KPMG

10

11 12

 14

13

McGill College

PROMENADES
DE LA
CATHÉDRALE

Sainte-Catherine

13

Galerie à
colonnade
du complexe
Les Ailes

14

Statue de
Maurice Richard

Empruntez maintenant l'escalier mobile pour atteindre le niveau Mezzanine, où se trouve une statue de **Maurice Richard *The Rocket*** intitulée *Ne jamais abandonner* (1999-2001) – la devise du grand joueur – de **Jean-Raymond Goyer** et **Sylvie Beauchêne**. Ce légendaire hockeyeur a permis aux Canadiens de Montréal de remporter huit coupes Stanley, un exploit que nous ne reverrons pas de sitôt! Un peu plus loin, examinez sur les colonnes de la galerie adjacente les reproductions d'anciennes photos noir et blanc relatant une part de l'histoire manufacturière de Montréal.

Descendez ensuite au niveau Métro et dirigez-vous à nouveau vers le Centre Eaton, à droite. Vous croiserez une succursale Signature de la **Société des alcools du Québec** (SAQ) qui propose une vaste sélection de vins et spiritueux et dont le cellier est

14

aménagé dans l'ancienne voûte d'une banque. Vous avez envie d'un rare cognac ? Vous trouverez à vous satisfaire. À moins que vous ne préfériez miser sur un produit des terroirs québécois et canadiens, tels caribous, vins, liqueurs d'érable, cidres de glace ou de feu et autres enivrants délices. N'hésitez pas à demander conseil !

■ Centre Eaton

De retour au Centre Eaton, descendez l'escalier mobile, à gauche, jusqu'au niveau Tunnel et empruntez, derrière l'escalier, le passage menant à la **place Ville-Marie**. Il a fallu attendre plus de quinze ans après la construction de ce tunnel pour qu'il devienne accessible au public. C'est que les propriétaires privés des immeubles doivent s'entendre sur les questions d'entretien, de sécurité et d'accessibilité des corridors. Pourtant, ce tronçon était critique, car il vient compléter le lien piétonnier entre les lignes de métro orange et verte ainsi qu'entre les gares de train et d'autobus.

Au bout du long couloir, montez l'escalier mobile pour accéder à la galerie de la place Ville-Marie. Retournez-vous pour jeter un coup d'œil à l'extérieur ; de ce point, on peut voir le temps qu'il fait !

■ Place Ville-Marie

Avancez jusqu'au prochain carrefour.

Si vous empruntez plutôt l'escalier mobile directement devant vous, vous pourrez faire une petite boucle pour admirer le hall sobre, mais imposant et les œuvres d'art de cet édifice iconique.

15

Reflet de la place Ville-Marie

Enfilez l'allée de circulation principale, à droite, et arrêtez-vous à l'entrée de la foire alimentaire. Là, une grande verrière vous offre une **vue imprenable sur la tour principale de la place Ville-Marie**.

Ce complexe concrétise le rêve marchand des années 1960 de Montréal pour son centre-ville, et il a toute une histoire. Auparavant s'y trouvait une vaste tranchée destinée à accueillir les voies reliant à la gare Centrale le tunnel ferroviaire creusé sous le mont Royal en 1918. Le centre-ville fut ainsi défiguré pendant 30 ans avant que le **Canadien National (CN)** et **William Zeckendorf**, un promoteur américain, ne conviennent d'un plan d'aménagement : un ensemble surmonté d'une tour cruciforme maximisant la lumière et portant la signature de **Ieoh Ming Pei**, l'architecte qui créera plus tard la pyramide du Louvre à Paris. Inaugurée en 1962, la place Ville-Marie était alors le plus haut gratte-ciel du Commonwealth, et elle est rapidement devenue l'emblème de la ville✶.

Empruntez ensuite l'escalier adjacent qui permet d'aller à l'extérieur.

✶ Anecdote

Le maire Jean Drapeau a insisté pour que la place Ville-Marie porte un nom français. Le promoteur suggérait « centre de la Réforme » ou « place de la Renaissance », mais le maire a imposé le nom actuel du complexe en souvenir du premier nom de Montréal.

★ Une saga de noms

Terminé en 1958, l'hôtel Reine-Elizabeth compte parmi les premiers hôtels en Amérique du Nord à posséder des escaliers mécaniques, la climatisation centrale et le téléphone dans chaque chambre. Le gouverneur général du Canada s'est rendu en Angleterre pour demander à la Reine l'autorisation de donner son nom au nouvel hôtel, ce qui a soulevé l'ire des nationalistes québécois, lesquels préféraient le nom de Château Maisonneuve en mémoire du fondateur de la ville. Les pétitions et les tentatives d'influence du maire Drapeau n'ont cependant pas réussi à faire changer le nom de l'établissement.

16

Rose des vents

17

Autoportrait de **Nicolas Baier**

■ **Esplanade de la place Ville-Marie**

Vous déboucherez sur une vaste place publique granitique offrant une superbe **perspective sur l'avenue McGill College et le parc du Mont-Royal**. Vous y découvrirez une **rose des vents**, la sculpture de bronze *Présence féminine* (1972) de **Gerald Gladstone** ainsi qu'*Autoportrait* (2012) de **Nicolas Baier**, un cube de verre trempé contenant une table de conférence et divers objets de nickel chromé, soulignant le 50e anniversaire de l'immeuble.

Du côté sud, se trouve l'**hôtel Fairmont Le Reine-Elizabeth ★**, qui a accueilli plusieurs grandes personnalités dont la reine Elizabeth II, Indira Gandhi, Charles de Gaulle, Nelson Mandela, le dalaï-lama et, surtout, **John Lennon**, qui, en 1969, y a tenu son célèbre *bed-in* avec Yoko Ono pour protester contre la guerre du Vietnam et enregistré son grand classique *Give Peace a Chance*.

Le Montréal souterrain

21

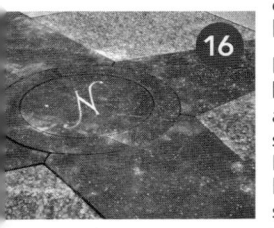

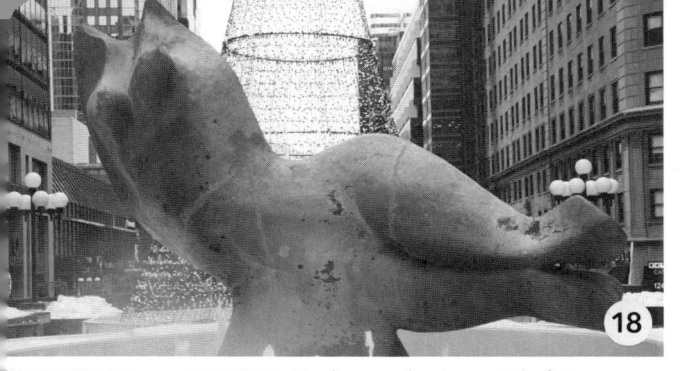

18

*Présence
féminine* de
Gerald Gladstone

19

Katz's
Delicatessen

Redescendez jusqu'à la foire alimentaire. Entre les escaliers se trouve dans un coin **Katz's Delicatessen**, un déli à l'ancienne et un comptoir express pour ceux qui aimeraient faire l'expérience intra-muros du célèbre *smoked meat* de Montréal, un plat de viande fumée d'origine juive. Poursuivez ensuite votre route en empruntant l'allée à droite en direction de la gare Centrale, dont vous atteindrez la galerie marchande après avoir descendu un escalier mobile.

■ Gare Centrale

Vous accédez ainsi aux halles de la gare. Suivez l'allée principale, où vous trouverez sûrement à vous restaurer. Vous serez d'ailleurs vraisemblablement tenté de le faire à la vue des comptoirs regorgeant de délices salés et sucrés de l'excellente **boulangerie Première Moisson**, une entreprise québécoise qui tente de mettre en valeur des produits locaux. Au bout de cette allée, vous déboucherez sur le vaste site principal de la gare.

Il s'agit du point d'origine du réseau souterrain, qui a par la suite entraîné la migration du district financier du Vieux-Montréal vers l'avenue

McGill College. La gare Centrale a été achevée en 1943, pendant la Seconde Guerre mondiale. Son aménagement devait s'inspirer du Rockefeller Center de New York, mais sous l'impulsion du courant moderniste, le résultat fut plutôt un cube de béton sans façade, un design révolutionnaire à l'époque qui a innové avec sa **salle des pas perdus** située au-dessus des trains et des quais, au même niveau que l'entrée des wagons. Aménagée dans le style paquebot, elle rappelle plus ce gros navire que le train ! L'œuvre *Monumental Frieze* de **Charles Comfort**, située aux deux extrémités, dépeint, à l'est, la vie au Canada, ses ressources nationales et ses industries, et à l'ouest, les loisirs et les libertés fondamentales. Elle est accompagnée d'extraits bilingues de l'*Ô Canada* de **Calixa Lavallée** et **Basile Routhier**, lequel a été interprété pour la première fois le 24 juin 1880, et choisi comme hymne national seulement un siècle plus tard.

C'est sur ces lieux très symboliques que se termine notre première balade. À partir de là, vous pouvez demeurer au centre-ville pour une visite extérieure, ou repartir en rejoignant le métro à proximité. C'est d'ailleurs là que débute la seconde balade. Pour y accéder, partez en direction du métro Bonaventure. Au bout d'un long couloir, traversez les portes vitrées afin d'emprunter le passage souterrain en descendant l'un des deux escaliers mobiles, puis suivez les panneaux indicateurs jusqu'à la station.

Gare Centrale

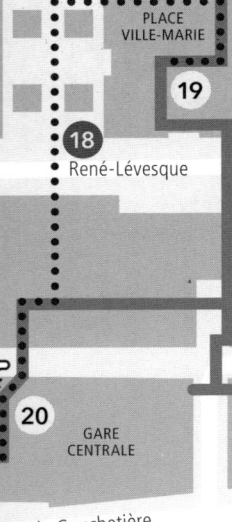

**BALADE 2
LE QUARTIER
INTERNATIONAL :
FOULÉES DANS
LES GALERIES DU
MONTRÉAL DESIGN**

DÉPART
Métro : station Bonaventure, place centrale

ARRIVÉE
Métro : station Place-d'Armes, place Jean-Paul-Riopelle

REPÈRES

ARCHITECTURE
Centre de commerce mondial de Montréal

ART
Place Jean-Paul-Riopelle

DIVERTISSEMENT
Patinoire du 1000 De La Gauchetière

RESTAURANT
Osco ! - Hôtel InterContinental Montréal

Cette randonnée s'inscrit dans l'axe est-ouest de la ville intérieure, plus récent, plus artistique et très design. Après le côté urbain et hypercommercial du centre-ville souterrain, j'apprécie ces espaces épurés aux ambiances diversifiées. On y entend le silence, l'esprit peut y faire le vide, et les yeux s'y reposer!

Le Quartier international est un ambitieux projet de revitalisation amorcé en 1999 qui a récolté plus d'une trentaine de prix et reconnaissances internationales. Il se veut la vitrine d'un Montréal branché et contemporain.

Allons-y!

Rendez-vous à la place centrale de la mezzanine du métro, près des panneaux d'affichage.

■ Station Bonaventure

Cette station achalandée est névralgique pour tout voyageur. Dépourvue d'art intégré, elle est elle-même une œuvre avec ses vastes proportions et ses profondes voûtes. C'est le point de départ de notre balade. Direction : le 1000 De la Gauchetière. De

Cathédrale

Mansfield

1

Métro Bonaventure

2

1000 DE LA GAUCHETIÈRE

Saint-Antoine Ouest

1

Station Bonaventure

2

Patinoire intérieure au 1000 De La Gauchetière

ce point, vous pourriez aussi, selon vos envies, partir dans la direction opposée pour visiter la gare Windsor et le Centre Bell à proximité.

En sortant de la station de métro, montez successivement deux escaliers mobiles.

■ **1000 De La Gauchetière**

Au-delà des portes tournantes de l'entrée, vous découvrirez immédiatement la principale attraction de l'immeuble, **L'Atrium Le 1000**, soit une **grande patinoire intérieure** accessible toute l'année. Regarder les patineurs aux habiletés variables est aussi amusant que d'y patiner soi-même.

3

Couloir
vers la place
Bonaventure

4

Le comptoir de
glaces artisanales
Fusion

5

Arrêt sur image de
Stéphane Pratte

3

4

5

Tournez à gauche après les portes, puis encore à gauche au couloir en direction de la place Bonaventure et de la rue de la Gauchetière pour atteindre l'entrée principale de l'édifice. En chemin, vous croiserez **Fusion**, un comptoir de glaces artisanales. L'estomac a toujours de la place pour une telle gâterie !

Dans le hall de verre de cette construction postmoderne de 1992, admirez l'installation ciné-tique *Arrêt sur image* de **Stéphane Pratte**, qui capte admirablement la lumière.

Montez à la mezzanine par l'esca-lier central pour mieux apprécier la vue de l'arrière de la **basilique-cathédrale Marie-Reine-du-Monde**, une petite réplique mon-tréalaise de la basilique Saint-Pierre de Rome et la résidence de l'arche-vêque catholique de Montréal. Vous constaterez que la verrière a été spécialement conçue pour que la perspective encadre son dôme.

Redescendez et dirigez-vous, à droite, vers la porte de côté marquée « Tunnel Bonaventure ». Après avoir descendu un escalier mobile, passez la porte à droite vers la place Bonaventure. Avancez jusqu'au prochain carrefour et

6

ue de l'arrière de la asilique-cathédrale Marie-Reine-du-Monde

7

Centre d'exposition de la Place Bonaventure

Le Montréal souterrain

6

7

tournez à droite, puis à gauche. Un escalier mobile ascendant vous mène à un immense centre d'exposition.

■ Place Bonaventure et Hôtel Hilton Montréal Bonaventure

Avancez vers l'entrée principale, près du kiosque de renseignements.

Vous reconnaîtrez, aux **murs de béton striés**, le style brutaliste des années 1960. Ce complexe est aménagé au-dessus des voies ferrées du centre-ville. Lors de son inauguration en 1967, il s'imposait comme le plus grand bâtiment commercial du monde, dépassant en superficie l'Empire State Building ! Plus d'un million de visiteurs visitent annuellement ses nombreux salons et expositions.

Suivez-moi ensuite jusqu'à un de mes endroits cachés préférés, les **terrasses-jardins de l'hôtel Hilton Montréal Bonaventure**. Vous l'atteindrez en empruntant le couloir à droite du kiosque de renseignements, puis en suivant les indications jusqu'à l'ascenseur : la réception est au 8e étage, le seul autre étage accessible. Là-haut, dirigez-vous vers la grande fenêtre qui livre un magnifique panorama sur le centre et le sud-ouest de la ville, le 1000 De La Gauchetière, la **basilique-cathédrale Marie-Reine-du-Monde** et le **fleuve Saint-Laurent** au fond à gauche. Dirigez-vous ensuite vers la réception de l'hôtel. Vous apercevrez des jardins rustiques, un ruisseau aménagé et la première **piscine chauffée extérieure** de Montréal – un délice

9

Marcello's

10

Rue University

en saison hivernale! N'hésitez pas à sortir, les curieux seront récompensés : des canards y passent l'hiver et le chef y tient son jardin de fines herbes. Ce petit détour vous dépaysera complètement. Gardez bien ce secret entre nous!

Faites le trajet à rebours pour revenir au kiosque de renseignements de la place Bonaventure et suivez le couloir principal, à droite, en direction de la **place de la Cité internationale**. En chemin, vous verrez les rénovations effectuées depuis 1998, notamment l'ajout de **panneaux lumineux aux tons rosés**, et vous croiserez **Marcello's**, un sympathique marché doublé d'un déli, ouvert en semaine seulement.

Au bout du corridor, empruntez l'escalier et dirigez-vous vers les grandes fenêtres qui offrent une belle **perspective sur la rue University** – un accès majeur au centre-ville – et d'où plusieurs édifices du Quartier international sont visibles. Notez l'important dénivelé de 45 mètres et la **colonnade aux couleurs des drapeaux internationaux** – 22 fûts de grandeurs différentes, mais d'égale altitude – révélant l'existence de plateaux. Les trottoirs devant les grands immeubles sont chauffants l'hiver, ce qui facilite les déplacements et évite les chutes! Ici, on a choisi des **lampadaires à double éclairage** conçus par **Michel Dallaire** qui diminuent astucieusement la pollution lumineuse.

9

10

11

Poursuivez en empruntant à gauche l'escalier le plus proche, de type « pas-de-cheval », puis un deuxième escalier en direction de la place de la Cité internationale afin d'accéder au **tunnel menant sous la rue University**.

Ce couloir quasi chirurgical appartient à l'Organisation de l'aviation civile internationale (OACI), qui permet la circulation, mais reste soucieuse de sécurité et préfère qu'on ne s'y attarde pas. Il se métamorphose toutefois en lieu d'exposition lors de l'événement **Nuit Blanche** du festival **Montréal en lumière**. Au bout du tunnel, deux escaliers mobiles ascendants vous mèneront à la surface.

11

Escalier de type « pas-de-cheval »

12

Tunnel

13

Galerie de l'OACI

14

Tour de la Bourse

■ **Organisation de l'aviation civile internationale (OACI)**

En franchissant les portes, vous vous trouverez dans une **immense galerie** avec une vue sur les drapeaux – dont celui de l'ONU, rappelant la vocation internationale du quartier – et sur la **Tour de la Bourse**, un édifice brun très sobre aux coins bétonnés construit en 1965 et abritant le siège de la Bourse des produits dérivés et de l'International Air transportation Association (IATA)*.

12

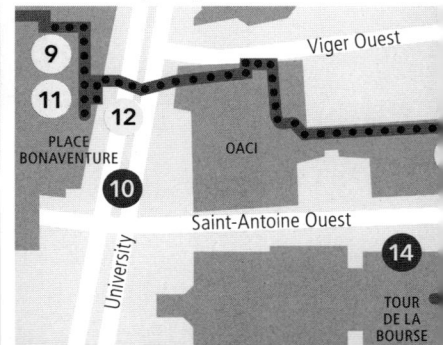

Avec un peu de chance, vous apercevrez, au 32ᵉ étage de la Tour de la Bourse, un couple de faucons pèlerins. Ce rapace de taille moyenne, réputé le plus rapide du monde en vol piqué, se nourrit d'oiseaux et de petits animaux terrestres. Il ne construit pas de nid, et il se perche toujours sur des structures élevées.

Rendez-vous au bout de la galerie, puis descendez l'escalier du hall d'entrée vitré donnant directement sur le square Victoria pour atteindre le couloir qui conduit à la station de métro éponyme. Après l'avoir franchi, sortez par la bouche de métro « à la parisienne », à droite.

■ **Square Victoria**

L'entrée de métro d'Hector Guimard est la seule de ce type en dehors de Paris. Datant de 1900 et de style Art nouveau, elle a été offerte à Montréal pour l'ouverture de son métro en 1966, un *prêt dont la durée devait se perdre dans la nuit des temps…* La rumeur veut que Paris ait tenté de la récupérer, n'en ayant plus d'aussi bien préservée. En échange, la Société de transport de Montréal a offert au métro de Paris, en 2011, l'œuvre de la photographe Geneviève Cadieux *La Voix lactée*, qui représente des lèvres de femmes – pour nous, c'est de l'Art *bécot*! Bref, vous pourrez ici admirer le caractéristique **carrelage blanc** et la **frise bleue** ornant la sortie, les dimensions et les escaliers exactement reproduits, le **garde-corps en fonte** aux motifs de serpents

15

L'entrée de métro d'Hector Guimard

16

Statue de la reine Victoria

et de végétaux, l'**enseigne « Métropolitain »**, les **lampadaires globuleux** et les **trois globes** qui éclairent l'escalier.

Le square, un ancien marécage asséché qui a connu diverses vocations, dont celles de marché à foin et de place commémorant le démantèlement des fortifications, a été renommé en 1860 en l'honneur de la reine Victoria à l'occasion d'une visite du prince de Galles pour l'inauguration du pont Victoria. En 1872, Lord Dufferin y dévoila une grande **statue de la Reine**, et une malveillante rumeur veut que ce soit en fait sa sœur plus jolie qui en ait été le modèle. Depuis le récent

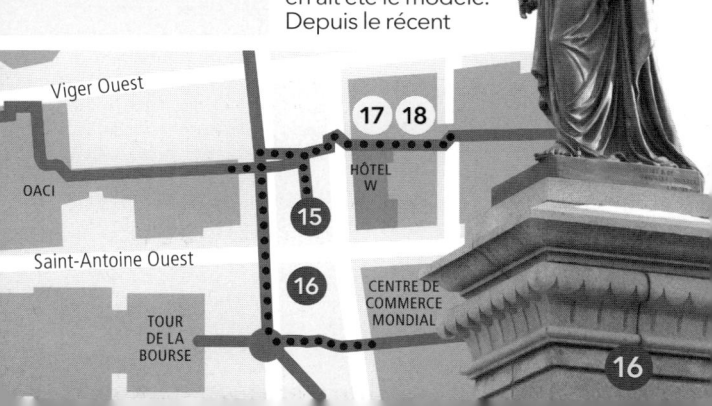

17
Couloir sous l'hôtel W

18
Stratifications pariétales de l'artiste montréalais Christian Kiopini

réaménagement du square, on y retrouve de nombreux arbres, des terrasses parsemées de sculptures modernes, des jets d'eau et des **bancs signés Michel Dallaire**. Remarquez, de l'autre côté de la rue, **l'entrée bleue de l'hôtel W** et les blasons des provinces au milieu des grandes fenêtres du bas, qui témoignent de son ancienne vocation de **Banque fédérale du Canada**.

Retournez dans le souterrain et empruntez le couloir blanc à droite pour une petite boucle.

■ Couloir sous l'hôtel W Montréal

Ce chic passage du Quartier international arbore des murs brillants bien éclairés et une touche de bleu, la couleur de l'hôtel W, dont c'est le soubassement. Au bout du couloir, remarquez les traces d'armature de l'ancien coffre-fort de l'édifice. Dans ce passage, vous trouverez *Stratifications pariétales* (2002-2003) de l'artiste montréalais **Christian Kiopini**, une œuvre géométrique en trois tableaux qui jouent sur les thèmes de la géologie, du souterrain et de l'ancienne vocation du lieu. Les strates de terre et les époques sont paradoxalement représentées en bleu, soit la couleur du fleuve.

19

La rotonde du square Victoria

Revenez sur vos pas en direction du métro Square-Victoria en descendant un escalier mobile, puis prenez à gauche en suivant l'indication du Centre de commerce mondial. Vous déboucherez alors sur la rotonde.

■ **La rotonde**

La **rotonde du square Victoria** est un espace de convergence avec un surprenant effet d'écho. Tenez-vous sur le **losange noir** tracé par terre au centre, et laissez votre inspiration s'exprimer. C'est pour moi l'occasion de sortir mon meilleur répertoire !

À partir de là, empruntez l'accès marqué « Centre de commerce mondial » par un **sinueux couloir de briques** dont les formes, les couleurs et les positions ont été variées pour créer des textures. En

20

Couloir sinueux

21

Centre de commerce mondial de Montréal

passant les portes, montez l'escalier mobile pour accéder à un spectaculaire atrium.

■ **Centre de commerce mondial de Montréal**

Notre World Trade Center, le **Centre de commerce mondial de Montréal**, est un complexe immobilier joignant les côtés de l'ancienne **ruelle des Fortifications** . Lieu transformé au début des années 1990, il a su conserver son cachet historique bien que le plafond soit constitué de verrières modernes. Son enceinte recèle de multiples trésors, notamment :

• un **édifice neuf en pierre grise** d'allure ancienne abritant l'empire de **Power Corporation** du regretté **Paul Desmarais** ;

✱ **Note historique**

La ruelle des Fortifications correspond à l'emplacement des remparts nord de la ville fortifiée, terminés en 1730. La ville croissant rapidement, on a procédé à leur démantèlement entre 1804 et 1812, et depuis cent ans, la ruelle est redevenue la voie de desserte des bâtiments

de la haute finance de la rue Saint-Jacques.

22
Bassin
en granit noir

23
Sculpture
d'Amphitrite
du sculpteur
Dieudonné-
Barthélemy
Guibal

- un monumental **bassin en granit noir** sur lequel coule un filet d'eau, fragile et miroitant, à l'image de la finance;

- de magnifiques **lampadaires** ornant la place;

- une **fontaine décorée d'une gracieuse sculpture d'Amphitrite**, épouse de Poséidon, réalisée par le sculpteur français **Dieudonné-Barthélemy Guibal** et acquise par Paul Desmarais auprès d'un antiquaire européen.

Empruntez l'escalier derrière la statue et traversez la première passerelle à droite, au bout de laquelle vous enfilerez le couloir immédiatement à gauche donnant sur l'entrée du très chic restaurant **XO de l'hôtel Le Saint-James**. Vous y trouverez des murales peintes rappelant que l'édifice a déjà accueilli Nordheimer, une entreprise réputée dans la fabrication de pianos.

Franchissez ensuite la prochaine passerelle pour atteindre le lobby de l'hôtel **InterContinental Montréal**. Vous trouverez là deux chaleureux établissements : **Osco!**, une brasserie aux accents de Provence dirigée par le chef **Matthieu Saunier** où l'on vous offre

**Restaurant
XO de l'hôtel
Le Saint-James**

en entrée baguette et tapenade,
et **Sarah B.**, un étonnant bar à
absinthe.

Ressortez du hall et descendez
l'escalier mobile. « Mais de quoi sont
recouverts les murs ? » vous deman-
derez-vous en les examinant de plus
près. De **vison véritable** et d'écorce
de bouleau, pour un effet saisissant!

Au bas de l'escalier, tournez à
gauche et poussez l'une des
portes devant vous pour retrouver
l'atrium principal près d'un **morceau du mur de Berlin**, quelques
pas à droite, un cadeau reçu par
Montréal en 1992 à l'occasion de
son 350ᵉ anniversaire et dont vous
pourrez lire les détails historiques.

Par la suite, revenez sur vos pas
et poursuivez vers l'escalier à
l'extrémité du complexe, sous la

**Mur recouvert de
vison et d'écorce
de bouleau**

**Morceau du mur
de Berlin**

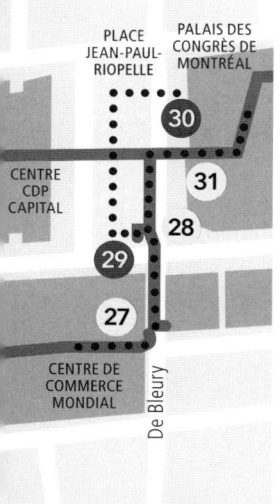

PLACE JEAN-PAUL-RIOPELLE
PALAIS DES CONGRÈS DE MONTRÉAL
CENTRE CDP CAPITAL
CENTRE DE COMMERCE MONDIAL
De Bleury

30
31
28
29
27

verrière inclinée à 45°, pour découvrir l'œuvre *Circulations* (2012) de **Rafael Sottolichio**, une murale colorée représentant le centre et soulignant son 20ᵉ anniversaire.

Empruntez la porte donnant sur un espace consacré au **musée d'archéologie et d'histoire de Montréal Pointe-à-Callière**. Arrêtez-vous un instant pour admirer la murale *Sous la ville d'aujourd'hui se cache un Montréal souterrain où se côtoient l'ancien et le nouveau* (2003) représentant les canaux et les rivières cachées de la ville, de nos jours souvent remplacés par des passages!

Juste en face, passez la porte menant au couloir en direction du Palais des congrès. Vous y verrez successivement une œuvre

27

Circulations de **Rafael Sottolichio**

28

Tables de **Michel Goulet**

29

Le Grand Jean-Paul de **Roseline Granet**

27

photographique intitulée *Sommeil (ou les séjours sous terre)* (2005-2006) d'**Isabelle Hayeur**, qui se veut une réflexion sur la consommation, et le diptyque *Tables* (2005) de **Michel Goulet**, constitué de deux panneaux gravés de drapeaux et de pictogrammes universels, symbolisant le caractère international du quartier, ainsi que d'une de ses célèbres chaises, bel exemple d'art symbolique et fonctionnel, quoique peu confortable ! Une œuvre qui se prête fort bien à un jeu de devinettes avec mes groupes de visiteurs.

Enfilez ensuite, juste en face, l'escalier qui mène à la surface pour une sortie sur la **place Jean-Paul-Riopelle**, aménagée sur la tranchée couverte de l'autoroute Ville-Marie.

■ Place Jean-Paul-Riopelle

Immédiatement, le bronze grandeur nature *Le Grand Jean-Paul* (2003) de **Roseline Granet** attire l'attention✱. À l'autre extrémité du parc se trouve *La Joute* (1969), une fontaine intégrant une œuvre de Riopelle en douze sculptures qui rend hommage à la nature et aux Premières nations. Vous

✱ Note biographique

Jean-Paul Riopelle est un Montréalais d'origine et un artiste connu mondialement. Entré à l'École du meuble de Montréal dans les années 1940, il y rencontra Paul-Émile Borduas. En 1948, il signe avec 14 autres peintres automatistes québécois le manifeste *Refus global*. Après la Seconde Guerre mondiale, il s'installe en France et fréquente André Breton, Alberto Giacometti et Samuel Beckett. Il revient au Québec au début des années 1990 et meurt en 2002 à l'Île-aux-Grues.

y découvrirez des silhouettes d'indien, d'ours, de chiens et de hiboux. Le tout s'anime en saison estivale.

Remarquez aussi l'élégant **Centre CDP Capital**, qui accueille les bureaux montréalais de la Caisse de dépôt et placement du Québec, une construction primée remplie d'innovations. Le centre abrite en outre le restaurant de haute gastronomie **Toqué!** du chef-propriétaire **Normand Laprise**, pionnier de la mise en valeur des produits québécois.

De l'autre côté du square se dresse la **façade de verre colorée du Palais des congrès** de l'architecte **Mario Saia** et son équipe. Dans le coin supérieur gauche, découvrez le volet extérieur du diptyque *Translucide* (2003), une œuvre collective représentant un visage et une main se touchant grâce aux jeux de lumière et d'ombre, et tenu pour être le plus **grand vitrail figuratif contemporain** en Amérique lors de son installation.

C'est avec ce florilège d'art que se termine notre balade dans le Montréal international souterrain, un dédale de couloirs qui

30

Façade de verre du Palais des congrès de Montréal

procurent toute une expérience esthétique. Les promoteurs du Quartier international ont réussi à créer une image de cité raffinée et contemporaine.

Vous pouvez traverser la rue et entrer directement au 1001, **place Jean-Paul-Riopelle** pour vous retrouver dans le hall de la place et du Palais des congrès. C'est de là que débutera la troisième balade. Si vous préférez passer par l'intérieur, rebroussez chemin jusqu'au couloir où se trouvent les œuvres de Goulet et continuez tout droit jusqu'à ce qu'il rejoigne le passage sous le Centre CDP Capital, que vous emprunterez à droite. Au bout, tournez à gauche dans un couloir aux coloris contrastés jaune et noir, et montez l'escalier mobile à gauche. Vous arrivez au Palais des congrès d'où vous pourrez rejoindre le hall de la place Jean-Paul-Riopelle, juste à côté.

■ **Palais des congrès**

De ce point, pour vous rendre au **métro Place-d'Armes**, suivez le couloir principal jusqu'au bout; il y a plusieurs indications. Vous pourrez, si le cœur vous en dit, sortir de la station pour explorer le **Quartier chinois** ou le **Vieux-Montréal** tout près.

Le Montréal souterrain

43

BALADE 3
QUARTIER DES
SPECTACLES :
À PAS COUVERTS
VERS LE MONTRÉAL
CULTUREL

DÉPART

Métro : station Place-d'Armes, 1001, place Jean-Paul-Riopelle – Palais des congrès

ARRIVÉE

Métro : station Place-des-Arts, place des Festivals

REPÈRES

ARCHITECTURE

Atrium – complexe Desjardins

ART

Foyer – Place des Arts

Espace culturel Georges-Émile-Lapalme

DIVERTISSEMENT

Musée d'art contemporain de Montréal

RESTAURANT

Place Deschamps – Place des Arts

Dans cette balade, nous explorerons l'axe nord-sud secondaire du RÉSO, qui conduit au cœur de la vie culturelle de Montréal. Nous emprunterons des couloirs d'apparence plus modeste que dans le Quartier international, mais les vastes espaces intérieurs aménagés et l'abondance d'ouvertures transforment ici la ville intérieure de sorte qu'on ne la perçoit plus comme aussi souterraine. Cette visite vous convaincra que le Montréal d'en dessous est une réalisation vraiment exceptionnelle.

■ Palais des congrès

Notre périple débute dans le hall ouest du Palais des congrès, un centre de conférences et d'expositions construit au-dessus de l'autoroute Ville-Marie à partir d'un édifice

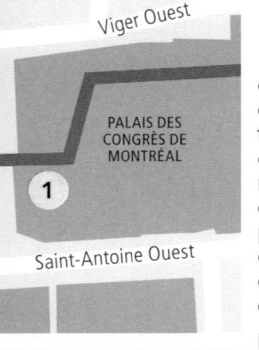

Viger Ouest

PALAIS DES
CONGRÈS DE
MONTRÉAL

1

Saint-Antoine Ouest

1

a constellation des
grands Montréalais

datant des années 1970. Inauguré en mai 1983, il a fait l'objet d'importants travaux d'aménagement et d'agrandissement au tournant du millénaire afin d'en doubler la capacité d'accueil. Il compte aujourd'hui parmi les centres les plus occupés d'Amérique du Nord, et accueille chaque année un grand nombre de congrès internationaux.

Dans le **hall Place Riopelle**, le long de la rue Saint-Antoine, vous apercevrez une **grande murale bleue** intitulée *La constellation des grands Montréalais* (2012) et regroupant plus d'une centaine de personnalités qui ont marqué la scène montréalaise, chacune représentée par un point lumineux et un symbole indicatif du domaine dans lequel elle s'est illustrée : culturel, économique, scientifique ou social.

1

2

Nature légère de
Claude Cormier

3

Noobox

Prenez le temps de repérer ceux de
ces grands Montréalais que vous
connaissez.

Près de ce hall, vous remarquerez
inévitablement la surprenante
forêt rose *Nature légère* (2002)
de **Claude Cormier**, constituée
de 52 troncs en béton reproduits
d'après de véritables arbres cente-
naires bordant l'avenue du Parc à
Montréal. La couleur en est inspirée
d'une teinte de rouge à lèvres en
référence à l'industrie cosmétique
locale, et elle symbolise la joie de
vivre si caractéristique de Montréal.

Longez ensuite le large corridor,
où vous trouverez boutiques et
comptoirs de restauration rapide
dont **Noobox**, qui propose un sympathique et économique concept
de plats asiatiques frais présentés

4

Passerelle surplombant l'avenue Viger

dans une boîte distinctive. Rejoignez l'entrée du métro Place-d'Armes en suivant les indications menant au **hall Viger**. Il s'agit d'une station peu profonde de Montréal, car elle repose sur l'ancien site de la rivière Saint-Martin, aujourd'hui canalisée. À proximité, montez l'escalier mobile menant à une passerelle et suivez les indications vers le complexe Guy-Favreau.

■ **Passerelle surplombant l'avenue Viger : vues du Vieux-Montréal et du Quartier chinois**

Le Montréal souterrain se fait ici aérien. Arrêtez-vous pour admirer le paysage des environs de l'avenue Viger, hommage toponymique au premier maire de Montréal, Jacques Viger (1833-1836). À votre droite, vous verrez :

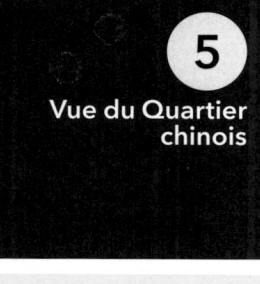

5

Vue du Quartier chinois

- l'élégante silhouette du **pont Jacques-Cartier**, inauguré en 1930 et d'abord baptisé pont du Havre;

- l'enseigne-horloge de la **brasserie Molson**, effervescente entreprise québécoise;

- la tour gris clair du nouveau **Centre hospitalier de l'Université de Montréal** (CHUM);

- la brique jaune, la porte d'entrée en angle et les toits en pagodes de l'**hôtel Holiday Inn** du Quartier chinois : un ensemble inspiré par l'art Feng shui;

- le **centre communautaire de la Mission catholique chinoise du Saint-Esprit** aux fenêtres octogonales, où sont donnés des cours de langue chinoise et de tai chi.

Ici, vous avez le choix de continuer à l'intérieur jusqu'au complexe Guy Favreau ou de sortir quelques instants pour découvrir une place très accueillante du **Quartier chinois**.

Si vous choisissez l'air frais, empruntez la sortie extérieure à votre gauche et débouchez derrière le complexe Guy-Favreau. Sinon, passez outre les consignes suivantes.

Petite place du Palais des congrès

Cette brève sortie vous fera découvrir un agréable espace urbain. À gauche, l'**église de la Mission catholique chinoise du Saint-Esprit** en pierre grise (1834-1835) s'impose comme l'un des plus anciens lieux de culte encore debout à Montréal, après avoir eu plusieurs vocations successives au fil de ses propriétaires écossais, français, slovaques, chinois et autres.

Maison Wing

De l'autre côté, repérez la **maison Wing** (1826), le plus vieux bâtiment du quartier, érigé par l'entrepreneur écossais **John Redpath** puis transformé en manufacture de nouilles et de biscuits en 1910. Les premiers **biscuits de *fortune* bilingues** ont d'ailleurs sûrement fait la fortune de leur créateur, **Arthur Lee**! Présentez-vous au 1009, rue Côté pour les déguster et connaître votre avenir. Je vous garantis que les messages sont toujours positifs, quoique pas toujours compréhensibles!

■ **Complexe Guy-Favreau**

À l'intérieur du complexe, le **couloir percé de puits de lumière** et bien gardé vous fera comprendre qu'il s'agit d'un édifice gouvernemental. Il s'y trouve plusieurs bancs où se rassemblent les aînés de la communauté chinoise. Presque au bout du couloir, empruntez le premier escalier mobile jusqu'au rez-de-chaussée, où vous découvrirez une **jolie cour extérieure** avec plusieurs variétés d'arbres, dont de magnifiques **Ginkgo biloba**.

Faites le tour du vaste **atrium du complexe Guy-Favreau** afin d'atteindre les escaliers de l'autre

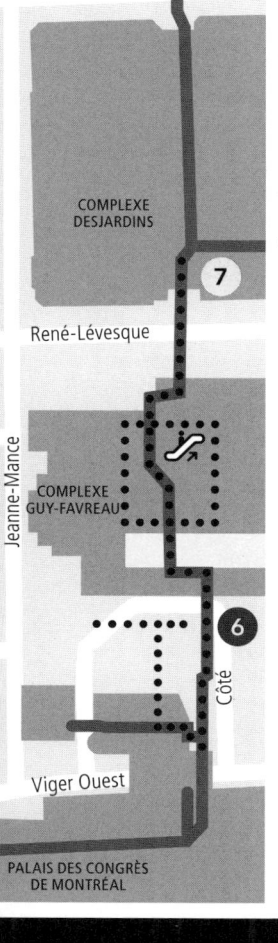

côté. L'immeuble où vous vous trouvez a été bâti en 1984 – après de longues tergiversations du gouvernement fédéral – sur l'ancien square Dufferin, lieu de réunion des membres de la communauté juive lui-même aménagé sur le site d'un ancien cimetière protestant (1799-1847). Il comporte d'immenses verrières et devait en principe offrir une vue ouverte de la **Place des Arts** à la **place d'Armes**. On imagine aisément la rivalité avec le complexe voisin, également doté de telles verrières. Dans l'entrée principale trône le **buste en bronze de Guy Favreau**, homme politique et juge canadien, portant cette citation : « La tolérance est la condition de la dignité même des hommes et de leurs cultures », toujours d'actualité !

Descendez jusqu'au tunnel passant sous le boulevard René-Lévesque et menant au complexe Desjardins, auquel on accède par deux escaliers mobiles (un ascenseur permet aussi le transit).

 Anecdote

L'ensemble multifonctionnel du complexe Guy-Favreau, construit à la hâte avec des matériaux de moindre qualité, a commencé, quatre ans seulement après sa construction, à s'effriter sérieusement, ce qui aurait fait dire aux aînés chinois que les esprits de leurs ancêtres manifestaient leur désapprobation quant à l'érection de l'édifice sur d'anciens lieux de sépulture.

■ Complexe Desjardins

À l'entrée du complexe, vous trouverez à droite la **cordonnerie Desjardins**, avec son service de cirage de chaussures à la main et sa chaise traditionnelle, un métier en voie de disparition. Discutez avec le sympathique artisan ; il se fera un plaisir de vous dévoiler les arcanes de l'art de faire briller le cuir.

Montez ensuite l'escalier mobile afin d'accéder à la **grande place** autour de laquelle gravitent les commerces répartis sur deux étages. Construit en 1967, après la Révolution tranquille, et situé dans un secteur de la ville tradition-nellement francophone, le complexe est un symbole de l'essor des Canadiens français en Amérique.

Le Montréal souterrain

53

7

Service de cirage de chaussures de la cordonnerie Desjardins

7

Complexe Desjardins

Il abrite les bureaux administratifs d'une coopérative financière fondée par **Alphonse et Dorimène Desjardins** en 1900. En date de son inauguration, sa forme octogonale était une première en Amérique du Nord. La conception du complexe, avec ses **deux immenses verrières** qui l'inondent de lumière naturelle, reflète avant tout la volonté du maire Jean Drapeau que la Place des Arts et les clochers de la basilique Notre-Dame soient visibles depuis son centre. La construction ultérieure du Palais des congrès a cependant obstrué la vue.

Le *Kynégraph* (2012) d'**Olivier Dufour**, un artiste québécois reconnu mondialement, et d'un collectif de plus de 200 autres artistes, se veut le point de mire de la grande place. Laissez-vous prendre à la

contemplation de ses jeux d'eau. Pendant la saison des fêtes, des décorations féériques et la présence du *vrai* **père Noël** font la joie de tous. Croyez-moi sur parole !

Furetez autour de la place dans les commerces qui la jouxtent : offrez-vous une petite douceur, achetez un livre… Vous y trouverez assurément votre bonheur. Je vous suggère notamment un arrêt à **La boulangerie moderne**, pour la fraîcheur et le raffinement de ses produits, et à **L'Art des artisans du Québec**, une belle vitrine pour plus de 150 artistes locaux.

Si, d'aventure, vous vous trouvez là à l'heure de l'apéro, montez au 6e étage et découvrez le **bar-salon de l'hôtel Hyatt Regency**, un régal accessible et peu connu du public. Et si c'est l'été, n'hésitez pas à profiter de la terrasse sur le toit.

Continuez ensuite jusqu'au couloir sous la rue Sainte-Catherine en suivant les indications vers le métro Place-des-Arts.

■ **Place des Arts**

À la sortie du tunnel, montez l'escalier mobile afin de rejoindre l'étage principal.

Dans le foyer, vous trouverez un sympathique bar à vin nommé **Place Deschamps** en l'honneur d'**Yvon Deschamps**, cet humoriste québécois adulé du public et habitué de la Place des Arts. L'endroit est tout indiqué pour prendre un verre et partager quelques bouchées avec des amis avant un spectacle. Juste à côté se trouve *Comme si le temps… de la rue*

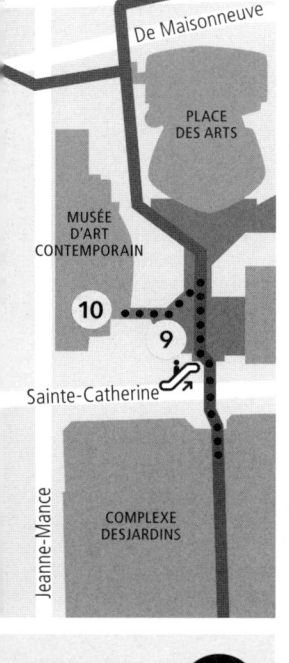

De Maisonneuve

PLACE DES ARTS

MUSÉE D'ART CONTEMPORAIN

10

9

Sainte-Catherine

Jeanne-Mance

COMPLEXE DESJARDINS

(1992) de **Pierre Granche**, évoquant la forme d'un théâtre antique et reprenant la trame de la ville du fleuve Saint-Laurent au mont Royal, le tout agrémenté de sculptures blanches en aluminium parfois comparées à des totems ou à des cariatides.

Un peu plus loin, vous trouverez l'entrée du Musée d'art contemporain de Montréal et sa boutique, directement reliés au Montréal souterrain. Je vous invite à explorer l'un et l'autre. La boutique regorge d'objets choisis de créateurs originaux et le musée est tout simplement extraordinaire !

■ **Musée d'art contemporain de Montréal (MACM)**

Fondé en 1964, il s'agit du premier musée canadien entièrement consacré aux œuvres contemporaines québécoises et internationales réalisées après 1939. Vous y verrez entre autres la plus importante collection de tableaux de **Paul-Émile Borduas**. L'intérieur d'une grande esthétique s'organise autour d'un magnifique **hall circulaire**.

Prenez tout votre temps, puis revenez vers le foyer.

9

Comme si le temps... de la rue de Pierre Granche

10

**Entrée du
Musée d'art
contemporain de
Montréal**

■ Place des Arts

Si ce lieu existe, c'est grâce à la ténacité de gens influents qui se sont regroupés autour du **maire Jean Drapeau** (encore lui!) afin de doter Montréal d'infrastructures culturelles modernes et de calibre international. Les travaux ont débuté en 1961 et la grande salle a été inaugurée en septembre 1963 par un concert notamment dirigé par **Wilfrid Pelletier**, en l'honneur de qui elle fut renommée en 1966. Claude Léveillée a été le premier artiste québécois à s'y produire en spectacle. **Les Grands Ballets canadiens** et l'**Opéra de Montréal** en ont également adopté la scène. Une grande quantité d'œuvres d'art s'y trouve par ailleurs, notamment *Amor*, huit hauts-reliefs de céramique réalisés par **Jordi Bonet**; ils symbolisent l'amour et la fécondité, et surplombent chacune des portes d'entrée de la salle. Mentionnons aussi des tapisseries des artistes **Micheline Beauchemin** et **Robert Lapalme**. Enfin, si vous avez l'occasion d'y assister à un spectacle, ne manquez pas de faire le tour des galeries et foyers.

Poursuivez votre visite en empruntant l'allée centrale, baptisée espace

11
Plafond de verre de Claude Bettinger

12
Salon urbain

culturel Georges-Émile-Lapalme, d'où vous pourrez profiter d'animations en tout genre, accéder à la salle d'exposition de la Place des arts – où se succèdent des événements thématiques à entrée libre – et observer l'amusant mur multimédia.

Au centre de cet espace, admirez *Plafond de verre* (1992) de **Claude Bettinger**, une œuvre qui ressemble à la fois à un télescope, à un kaléidoscope et à un périscope avec son ange pointant le ciel et visible tant de la galerie souterraine que de l'extérieur. Elle rappelle que « l'artiste est celui qui fait voir l'autre côté des choses ». Cette phrase est d'ailleurs inscrite dans l'œuvre ; saurez-vous la trouver ? Faites une petite boucle pour mieux apprécier l'ensemble en empruntant l'une des portes de côté – par lesquelles vous reviendrez – pour sortir sur l'**esplanade de la Place des Arts**, d'où vous jouirez d'une magnifique perspective : complexe Desjardins, **théâtre Maisonneuve**, **Maison symphonique**, **salle Wilfrid-Pelletier**, **Musée d'art contemporain**, aménagements et **lampadaires** caractéristiques des lieux, etc.

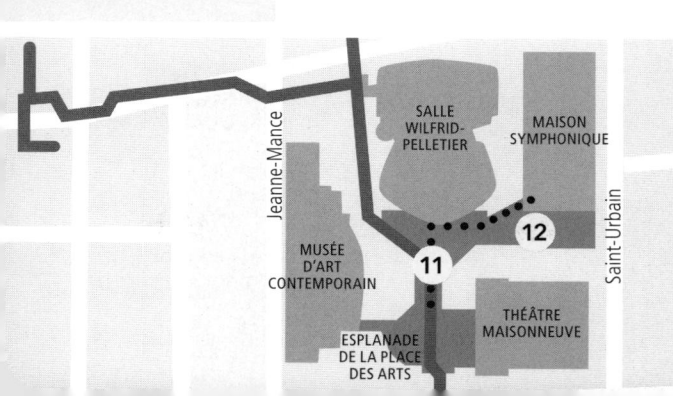

De retour à l'intérieur, dirigez-vous vers la rue Saint-Urbain. Vous y trouverez le **Salon urbain** caché derrière des rideaux rouges translucides, comme sorti d'un pliage d'origami! À ses côtés, le **Studio ARTV** et la **Maison symphonique de Montréal**, la plus récente salle de concert de la ville, où se produisent l'Orchestre symphonique de Montréal, l'Orchestre métropolitain, I Musici de Montréal, Les Violons du Roy et quelques autres ensembles. Son inauguration a eu lieu en septembre 2011, et elle serait, selon le chef **Kent Nagano**, la salle la mieux adaptée à la musique d'orchestre du monde. Son **grand orgue** fabriqué par la prestigieuse maison Casavant Frères de Saint-Hyacinthe comporte 109 registres, 83 jeux, 116 rangs et quelque 6489 tuyaux.

SALON URBAIN

13
Salle Wilfrid-Pelletier de la Place-des-Arts

14
La Cinquième salle de la Place-des-Arts

Rebroussez chemin et dirigez-vous vers la Cinquième salle et le métro Place-des-Arts. En chemin, vous croiserez le restaurant **Le Seingalt**, qui expose dans sa vitrine des **costumes des productions** présentées à la Place des Arts, et une succursale des magasins **Archambault**, un commerce québécois fondé en 1896 qui vendait traditionnellement des partitions de musique. Profitez-en pour jeter un coup d'œil aux affiches qui annoncent les spectacles à venir.

Passez deux séries de portes pour accéder à la station de métro.

■ **Station Place-des-Arts**

Immédiatement à l'entrée apparaît une immense **verrière rétroéclairée** et protégée par un verre renforcé

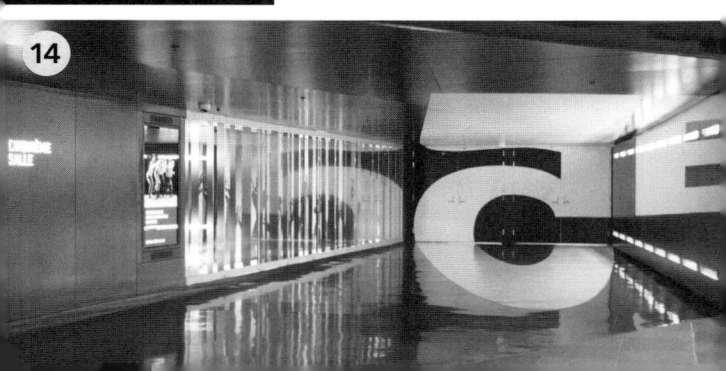

d'acier faisant miroiter les couleurs vives de *L'histoire de la musique à Montréal ou Les arts lyriques* (1967) de **Frédéric Back**. Y sont représentées des figures marquantes de la musique canadienne, dont **Calixa Lavallée**, **Guillaume Couture**, **Alexis Contant** et la soprano **Emma Albani**, et elle retrace le parcours de la musique traditionnelle autochtone à la musique innovatrice de l'âge moderne. Il s'agit de la première œuvre commanditée du métro – gracieuseté des supermarchés Steinberg.

Vous noterez aussi l'enseigne des **Étoiles du métro**, là où peuvent se produire les meilleurs musiciens publics spécialement sélectionnés par la Société de transport de Montréal (STM). Prenez le temps d'apprécier et d'encourager le talent qu'ils partagent avec bonheur. La musique est souvent présente dans le métro, et permise partout où vous voyez un panneau mural à l'**image d'une lyre**. Elle confère aux lieux un agréable cachet, surtout aux heures de pointe. Plaisir d'oreille assuré !

Empruntez ensuite l'escalier mobile à gauche des tourniquets pour atteindre la place des Festivals, ultime destination.

15

L'histoire de la musique à Montréal ou Les arts lyriques de **Frédéric Back**

15

■ Place des Festivals du Quartier des spectacles

Dès la sortie du métro, vous découvrez la **place des Festivals**, une place publique du Quartier des spectacles inaugurée en septembre 2009 qui borde la rue Jeanne-Mance en face du Musée d'art contemporain de Montréal. Son aménagement inclut **235 jets d'eau pulsés**, éclairés de rouge et de blanc, sous lesquels peuvent s'ébattre les enfants les jours de canicule, comme dans toutes les grandes villes du monde. C'est le site de prédilection des grands festivals montréalais : **Festival international de jazz**, **FrancoFolies**, **Juste pour Rire**, **Montréal en lumière**, etc. La place se transforme au fil des saisons et présente tous les hivers des installations interactives originales.

Goûtez quelques moments en cet agréable lieu, symbole culminant des efforts déployés par Montréal pour faire vivre la scène culturelle, avant de repartir vers de nouvelles découvertes.

C'est ainsi que s'achèvent nos déambulations à travers la ville souterraine et ses histoires. Je vous invite à refaire ces balades régulièrement, car les ambiances changent selon les heures, et les corridors s'animent au gré des saisons et des multiples événements qui ponctuent la vie montréalaise.

CONCLUSION

Le Montréal souterrain est un espace complexe fait d'ombre et de bouts de ciel. Cette ville intérieure s'étendra assurément pour relier de nouveaux espaces. Dans les décennies à venir, elle rejoindra sans nul doute les secteurs effervescents que sont, entre autres, le Quartier de la santé, le Quartier de l'innovation, la Cité du multimédia, Griffintown et d'autres encore, procurant ainsi l'occasion de nouvelles balades. Les travaux de l'Observatoire de la ville intérieure de l'Université de Montréal vous permettront de suivre son évolution : www.observatoiredelavilleinterieure.ca/.

Je vous souhaite encore beaucoup de plaisir et de nombreuses découvertes sur les sentiers abrités de Montréal dont vous savez désormais mieux capter l'essence. N'hésitez pas à m'en donner des nouvelles; un guide adore recevoir des commentaires!

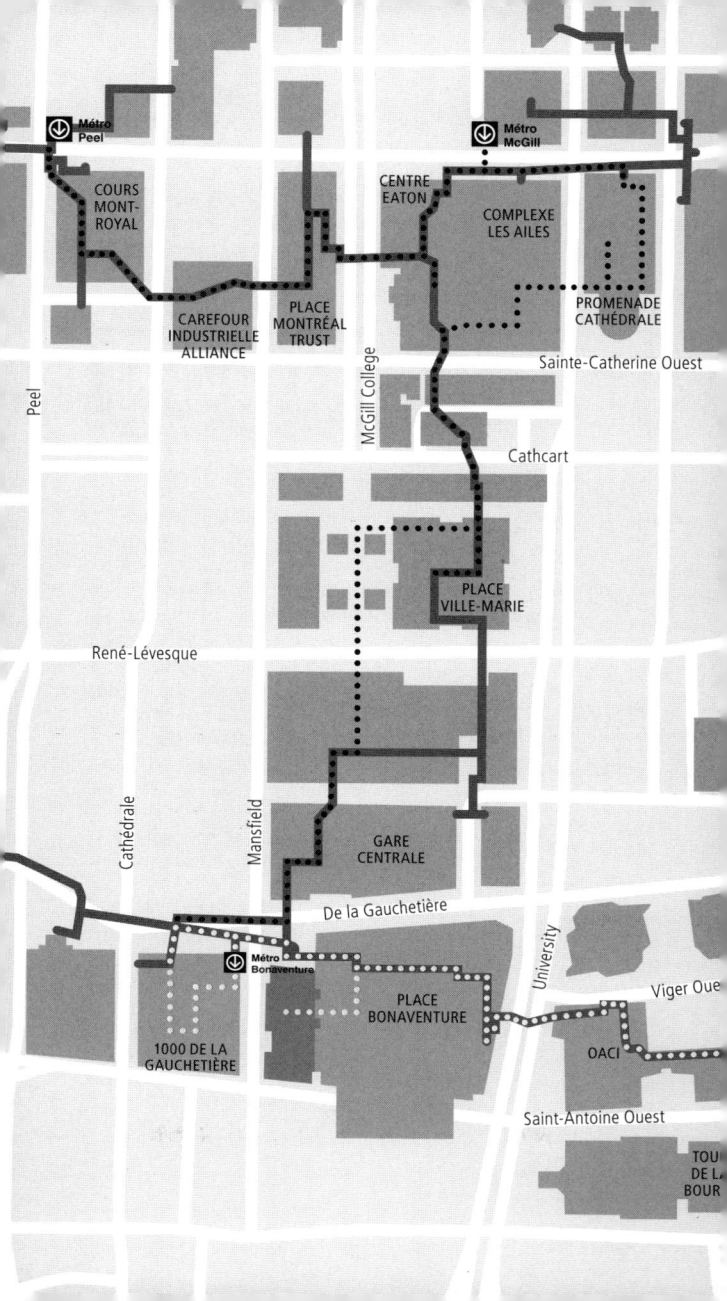